Alice Vansittart Carr

Margaret Maliphant

Vol. II

Alice Vansittart Carr

Margaret Maliphant
Vol. II

ISBN/EAN: 9783337041007

Printed in Europe, USA, Canada, Australia, Japan

Cover: Foto ©Andreas Hilbeck / pixelio.de

More available books at **www.hansebooks.com**

MARGARET MALIPHANT

A NOVEL

BY

MRS COMYNS CARR

AUTHOR OF 'LA FORTUNINA,' 'NORTH ITALIAN FOLK,' ETC.

IN THREE VOLUMES

VOL. II.

WILLIAM BLACKWOOD AND SONS
EDINBURGH AND LONDON
MDCCCLXXXIX

MARGARET MALIPHANT.

CHAPTER XV.

I GOT up the next morning just as usual.
Nothing should have induced me to confess
that there was anything the matter with me,
although my arm was so stiff that it was with
the greatest pain that I carried in the breakfast urn, and my head ached so from my fall
that it was hard enough to put a good face
upon it when mother remarked again upon
the disfigurement that I had upon my cheek.
But although I gave no sign, I was not used
to being ill, and it did not improve my temper.

Things were not comfortable in the house,
and I did nothing to make them better. To

VOL. II.   A

be sure, I kept my promise of talking to Reuben, but I'm afraid that I did not even do that in a manner to be of any use. I met Mr Harrod as I passed out into the stable-yard, and he asked me how I did. That alone put me out. To have been asked how I did by any one that morning would have annoyed me, but to be asked how I did by the man who was somehow connected with my doing ill, annoyed me specially. I fancied it would have been in better taste if he had not remarked upon a body's appearance when she was looking her worst; and anyhow, it seemed to me an unnecessary formality. I feel really ashamed now to write down such nonsense, but there is no doubt that these were my feelings at the time. I do not think that I even answered him by anything more than a "good morning," but passed on as though I had the affairs of the world on my shoulders.

I found Reuben rubbing down the mare who was to go into town with father. She neighed as I came in, and stretched out her neck. I had no sugar, but she licked my hand, nevertheless; and I remembered Reuben's compliment to me about my ability to win the love of beasts. It consoled me a little at a time when I thought I should always stand aloof, not only from the love but even from the comradeship of human beings. And it gave me courage to say what I wanted to say to Reuben. It was something to know that I was at least the old man's favourite.

"Reuben," I began, plunging boldly into the matter, "whatever made you behave so badly to father's bailiff when he came round the place?"

There had been a special cause of complaint that very morning when father had first taken Mr Harrod round the farm, so I had a handle upon which to begin.

"Don't you know," I went on, "that this gentleman has got to be master over you?"

"Master!" repeated Reuben, stopping his work, and looking straight at me; "no, miss, I knows nothing about that."

I had used the word on purpose to draw out the whole sting at once.

"Yes," continued I, "he's going to be father's bailiff."

"Bailiff!" repeated Reuben, again putting on his most stolid air. "I knows nothing about that."

"Well," explained I, trying neither to laugh nor to be annoyed, "that means that he is going to manage the land and give orders the same as father, so that there'll be two masters instead of one."

Reuben continued rubbing down the mare's coat till it began to shine like satin.

"I've heard tell," answered he at last, "there's something in the Book that says a man don't have no call to serve two masters."

This time I did laugh outright. "Oh, that's different, Reuben," said I, — "that's different; but these two masters will both be good, and both will want you to do the same thing."

"Do ye know that for sure, miss?" asked Reuben again, and I had a lurking suspicion that he did not ask in a perfectly teachable spirit. "I've heard tell as when there be two masters, they always wants a man to do just the opposite things."

I paused a moment. I did not know what

to answer, for it seemed to me as though there might be a great deal of truth in this.

But I said bravely, " Oh no, Reuben."

Reuben scratched his head. " Well, miss, Farmer Maliphant, he have been my master fifteen year come Michaelmas, and he have been a good master to me. Many another would have turned me away because o' the drink. It was chill work at times down there on the marsh when I was with the sheep, and the drink was a comfort. I nigh upon died o' the drink, but Farmer Maliphant he have been patient with me, and he give me another chance when others would have sacked me without a word. And now I be what parson calls a reformed character."

" Well, you are quite right to avoid drinking, Reuben," said I, chiefly because I did not know what to say.

" Yes ; but I don't mind tellin' you, miss," continued Reuben confidentially, " that farmer he have more to do with making a pious man of me than parson had : not but what I respec's the Church ; but bless you, parson wouldn't ha' given me nothing for giving up o' my bad ways, and where's the use of doing violence to yerself if ye ain't a-goin' to get nothing by it?"

Reuben wiped his brow. This long and unwonted effort of speech was almost too much for him.

"Nay, parson he didn't offer me no reward," added he, "but farmer he did. He says to me, 'Reuben,' he says, 'if you give up the drink you shall stay on as long as I'm aboveground;' and three times I backslided, I did, and three times he give me another chance; and now as I'm a respectable party, and a honour to any club as I might belong to, I means to stick to my old master, and not be for going after follerin' any other mammon whatsomever."

I brightened up at this declaration.

"Well, I'm glad of that, Reuben," said I. "I'm sure we none of us want you to leave us after all these years."

"Lord bless you, I ain't a-going to leave," answered he simply.

"Then that's all right," answered I. "If you have made up your mind to do as you're bid, I know father will be true to his word, and will never turn you off so long as he is alive."

"Ay, the master'll be true to his word," echoed the old man, nodding his head, "and I'll be true to mine, but I won't go follerin' after no new masters. One master's enough for me, and him only will I serve."

He gave the mare a smack upon her haunches, and turned her off; the light of reason faded from his face, and I knew that it was absolutely useless to say another word to him on the subject. I turned to go within; and in the porch, with a bowl in her hand, stood Deborah facing me, with an exasperating smile on her wide red face, and something more than usually aggressive in her broad strong figure. I looked round and saw that the gate of the yard was open, and that Mr Harrod, with his heavy boots and gaiters on, ready for work, stood just behind me. I could have cried with vexation.

"Mr Maliphant is waiting," said he, going up to the animal that Reuben had just finished harnessing, and fastening the last buckle himself. "I'll drive the cart round to the front myself." And he took the reins and jumped up, while Reuben, in gloomy silence, tightened one of the straps. I went and opened the gates, and with a nod of thanks to me, Mr Harrod dashed out.

I cannot tell whether it was the strap that he had fastened himself, or whether the one that had been Reuben's doing, but something galled the mare. She reared, and began to kick. Without a smile upon his face, and without moving an inch, Reuben said, " Ay, it takes a man to hold that mare."

" You fool!" cried I, quite forgetting my-self. " It isn't the man, it's the harness."

I flew down the gravel after the cart. The horse was still kicking violently. Every muscle of Mr Harrod's dark face was set in hard lines.

" Leave her alone," cried he, as I ap-proached; "don't touch her."

Something in his voice cowed me, and apparently cowed the horse also, for she was quiet in an instant, her sides only quivering with nervousness. I sprang to her and un-loosed the cruel strap. She turned to me, and I held her by the bridle and patted her neck. Mr Harrod got down and examined the cart. Fortunately it was not materially hurt.

"What can Reuben have been about to tighten that so," said I. "It was enough to madden any horse."

He did not answer.

"I'm afraid he was angry at your giving him an order," said I. "You must excuse him. He's an obstinate old fellow, but he is a good servant, and he has been with us many years."

"It's the most natural thing in the world that he should dislike me at first," answered Trayton Harrod, with that smile of his that was such a quick, short flash. "I rather like the sort of people who resent interference. But I don't suppose it was his doing for a moment. I buckled this up wrong."

He pointed to his part of the job. Father came up, and they drove off quietly together. I went back into the yard, musing on his words.

"I don't believe you'll find Mr Harrod an unjust master, Reuben," said I.

Reuben took no notice; but Deborah laughed, and said grimly—

" Well, he's a fine-grown young man, any-how; and he'll know how to drive a mare, I don't doubt."

But I paid no attention to her words. I was wondering why Mr Harrod had said that he rather liked people who resented interference.

CHAPTER XVI.

A FORTNIGHT passed. I had seen little or nothing of Mr Harrod till one afternoon when, with a volume of Walter Scott under my arm, I had taken my basket to get some plovers' eggs off the marsh. I had wandered a long way far beyond that part of the dyke that lay beneath the village and was apt to be frequented by passers-by, and I had already about a dozen eggs in my little basket, when I heard some one whistling down behind the reeds on the opposite side of the bank.

It might have been a shepherd. There was a track across the level here, and none but the shepherds knew it; but somehow I did not think it was a shepherd. I sat down upon the turf, for the bulrushes in the dyke had not yet grown to any height, and I did not want to be seen.

" Taff!" called a voice.

Yes, it was Mr Harrod. I had missed the St Bernard when I had been coming out, and had wondered where he had gone, for I had wanted him for a companion — Luck, the sheep-dog, being out with Reuben. I wondered how it was that Mr Harrod could have taken him.

I sat quite still among the rushes, where I had been looking for the birds' nests. I did not want to be seen, and, as far as I remembered, there was no plank over the dyke just here. But there was some one who knew the marsh better than I did. It was the dog. As soon as he got opposite to where I was, he began barking loudly, and then he ran back some hundred yards and stood still, barking and wagging his tail, and as plainly as possible inviting his companion to follow him.

Mr Harrod must have loved dogs almost as much as I did, for he actually turned back, and when he came to where Taff stood he laughed. There was evidently a plank there, and I suppose he must have guessed that he was expected for some reason to cross over.

He did so, and Taff followed. The dog tore
along the path to me, and Mr Harrod followed slowly. He did not seem at all surprised to see me. He came towards me with
a book in his hand.

" I think you must have dropped this," he
said, handing it to me. "We found it just
down yonder."

He said "we." It must have been the
sagacity of that wretched dog which had
betrayed me, for there was no name in the
book. I took it reluctantly : I was rather
ashamed of my love of reading. Girls in the
country were not supposed usually to be fond
of reading. If it hadn't been for those good
old-fashioned novels in father's library, mother
would have considered the Bible, and as much
news as was needed not to make one appear
a fool, as much literature as any woman re-
quired. A love of reading might be considered an affectation in me, and there was
nothing of which I had such a wholesome
horror as affectation.

I took the book in silence—my manners
did not mend—and stooped down to pat the
dog. I wanted to move away, but I didn't

quite know how to do it. Taffy wagged his tail as if he hadn't seen me for weeks. Foolish beast! If he was so fond of me, why did he go after strangers so easily?

"Taff knows the marsh," said I, for the sake of saying something.

"Famously," said Mr Harrod. "He shows me the way everywhere. We are the best of friends."

I frowned. Was it an apology for having taken my dog?

"Taff will follow any one," I said roughly.

It was not true, for Taff had never been known to follow any one before; and even as I said it, I wondered if Mr Harrod were one of those whom "the beasts love," but he took no notice of my rudeness.

"What have you got there?" asked he, looking into my basket.

"Plovers' eggs," answered I. "There are lots on the marsh nearer the beach."

"Lapwings' eggs," corrected he, taking one in his hand.

"Oh no! plovers' eggs," insisted I. "They are sold as plovers' eggs in the shops in town as well as here."

"Yes," smiled he. "They are sold as plovers' eggs all over the London market also, but the lapwing—or the pewit, as you call it—lays them for all that. It is a bird of the plover family, but it should not properly be called a plover."

I bit my lip.

"Of course those are not all plovers' eggs," said I, taking up one of a creamy colour spotted with brown, which was quite different to the grey ones mottled with black, that seemed to have been designed to escape detection on the grey beach, where they are generally found. "This is a dabchick's egg."

"I see you know more about birds than most young ladies do," said Mr Harrod; "but I should call that a moor-hen's egg. And as for the grey plover, it is a migratory bird; it does not breed in England."

I suppose I still looked unconvinced, for he added pleasantly, "Come, I'll bet you anything you like; and if we can be lucky enough to find a bird on the eggs, I'll prove it you now."

He turned round and began walking slowly along the bank of the dyke, close to the water's edge. I gave Taff a friendly cuff to keep him quiet, for he was rather excitable, and it was necessary that we should be very wary if we wanted to surprise the bird sitting.

Mr Harrod crept cautiously along, and I followed. I was as anxious now as he was, and by this simple means I was entrapped into a walk with my sworn enemy. A brown bird with a long bill got up among the reeds, and flew in a halting manner down to the water. It was a water-rail, and Mr Harrod said so—for these birds are rarer upon the dyke than the moor-hens and pewits, of which there are a great number, and I suppose he imagined I would not know it.

Something moved in the growing rushes at our feet; but it was only a couple of black moor-hen, who took to their heels, so to speak, with great velocity, and made little flights in the air with their legs hanging down and their bodies very perpendicular. We stood and laughed at them a minute, they were so very absurd out of their proper element; but when they took to the water they were pretty enough, the little red shields standing out upon their black foreheads as they jerked their heads in swimming.

I came upon a mother moor-hen presently tending her little brood; the large flat nest, built of dried rushes, lay in the overhanging branches of a willow-shrub, and she stood on the bank hard by. She did not fly or run away as other birds do when frightened, but stood there croaking as if in anger, and fluttering anxiously round the place where the six little balls of black down showed their red heads above the edge of the nest.

I held Taff by the collar, to prevent his doing any mischief, and we left the poor faithful mother undisturbed. We had not found any plovers' eggs since we had begun to look. They are always hard to find, being laid upon the open ground, sometimes on the very beach, where they almost look like little pebbles themselves, and sometimes in furrows and clefts of the earth, but always without any nest to mark the place. I suppose I had pretty well scoured this particular reach.

About a hundred yards farther on, how-

ever, the strange cry that distinguishes the
bird we sought fell upon our ears : a cock
lapwing flew up, his long feathery crest erect,
and tumbled over and over in the air in
the manner peculiar to his kind, uttering all
the while the plaintive " cheep, cheep " that
means distress and anxiety.

Mr Harrod held out a warning hand behind him as he crept forward gently on tip-
toe, and I was obliged to be silent, although
I was particularly anxious to speak.   Presently he beckoned to me to advance, and as
I did so I saw the hen-bird running along the
bank as close to the ground as possible, while
in a furrow close by my feet lay the pretty
grey-spotted eggs that we were looking for.

Mr Harrod turned and looked at me with
a little smile, which I chose to think was one
of triumph.   " That proves nothing," said I.
" I call that bird a plover—a green plover. I
can't help it if you call it something else. Of
course I know there's another sort of plover—
the golden plover ; but no one could confuse
the two, for this one has got a crest on its head
which it lifts up and down when it likes."

" Oh, I beg your pardon," answered he.

" I see you know all about it.   It's only a
confusion of terms."

I flushed, and stooped down to pick up the
eggs.

" No, don't," said he ; " let the poor thing
have them.   You will see, she will fly back
as soon as we have gone away."

We stepped back into the path, and
surely, in a moment, the two parents met in
the air, tumbling over together, and still
uttering their plaintive cry.   Then presently
the hen-bird floated down again and returned
to her patient duty ; and soon her mate followed her also, and both were hidden among
the rushes.

I turned round with a little laugh.   I had
thought I was annoyed, but the fact is, I was
too happy to be annoyed.

The panoply of a tender grey sky, fashioned of many and many soft clouds, floating
over and past one another, and lightening a
little where the sun should have been, was
spread over the placid ground : the sea was
grey, too, beyond the flats, melting into the
grey sky ; the white headland in the distance, and the grey towers along the shore,

seemed very near and distinct ; sheep wandered up and down the banks of the dyke,
cropping steadily ; the air was soft and kindly. My heart beat with a sense of satisfaction
that was unlike anything I had ever felt before ; and yet many was the time that I had
been out on the marsh on just such a soft
day, among the birds and the beasts whom I
loved.

"Listen," said I presently, breaking the
pleasant silence, as a loud, screaming bird's
note, by no means beautiful, but full of delightful associations, came across the marsh.
"The swifts are beginning to sing — that
means summer indeed."

A little company of the lovely black birds
came towards us, flying wildly in circles above
the dyke, sipping the water as they skimmed
its surface, and then away again over the
meadows.

"I wonder how it is that they are so black
and glossy when they come over to us, and
so grey and dingy when they go away,'
said I.

"Have you noticed that as a fact?" asked
he.

" Oh yes," I replied, and I am sure that I was very proud to be able to say so. " They come for May Day, looking as smart as possible ; and they don't look at all the better for their seaside season when they leave at the end of August."

" I expect they moult in those other countries to which they go when they leave us. But I haven't noticed very many swifts about here, anyhow. Perhaps the country is too wild for them."

" Well, we have plenty of swallows," said I, " and martins too. And I don't know why swifts should be so much more particular than the rest of their family. But I have a standing disagreement upon that point with our old servant Reuben. He swears that there are only eight pairs of swifts in the village, and that the same birds come back every year to the same place."

" That sounds rather incredible," said Mr Harrod.

" So I say," rejoined I. " But he insists that he has counted the pairs, and that they are always the same number. And as, of course, there must be a pair of young to every pair of old birds when they leave us, he argues that the parent birds refuse to allow the young ones to inhabit the same place when they return. Reuben is as positive about it as possible," added I, laughing. " These swifts live under the eaves of the old church ; and I do believe he greets them as old friends every year."

" I shouldn't venture to say that he was mistaken," said Mr Harrod. " So many curious things happen among beasts and birds; and swifts are particularly amusing creatures. Reuben appears to be quite a naturalist."

I had quite forgotten my self-imposed attitude of defiance in the keen interest of this talk ; but something in the tone of this remark roused it afresh.

" If that means some one who knows about birds and things, yes—he is," answered I, with a shake of my head,—a foolish habit which I know I had when I wanted to be emphatic. " Probably a much better naturalist than people who learn only from books. He taught me all I know," added I, proudly, and not for a moment perceiving the construction that might be put upon this remark. " I used to be out here with him whole days when I was a child, and we both of us got into no end of scrapes for doing what we ought not to do, and leaving undone what we had to do. Oh, but it was fun!" added I, with a sigh.

My companion laughed. " Delightful, I am sure," said he ; " and it did you a great deal more good than sticking to books, I'll be bound."

He looked at me straight as he said this, as though he were taking my measure.

" I did stick to my books too," cried I quickly, anxious that he should not think me an ignoramus. " Mother was always very particular about that."

" Yes, yes, of course," said he. And then he added, with what I fancied was a twinkle of fun in his eye, " ' The Fair Maid of Perth ' is not every young lady's choice."

I blushed. Perhaps, after all, he did not think me ridiculous for reading novels. I was half angry, half ashamed, but it never occurred to me to wonder why I should care what this new acquaintance said or thought.

"We didn't read novels in lesson-time,"
said I, stiffly; "we didn't read many novels
at all. Father and mother don't hold with
novels for girls, and mother don't hold with
poetry either, but father likes Milton and
Shakespeare."

"I daresay they are quite right," said my
companion. "But you are not of the same
mind, I suppose?"

"No," answered I, boldly, determined to
be honest. "I think Sir Walter Scott's
novels are lovely; and I like poetry—all that
I can understand."

Mr Harrod laughed. "I don't think I
should have been willing to admit there was
anything I couldn't understand when I was
your age," he said.

I looked at him surprised. He talked
as though he were ever so much older than
I was, although he did not look more than
six- or seven-and-twenty. I forgot that even
then there would be years between us. I
always was forgetting that I was scarcely
more than a child.

"I think that would be silly," said I, loftily.
I forgot another thing, and that was that I

had shown Mr Harrod pretty constantly since he had been at the Grange that I was not fond of admitting there was anything I could not understand, and that if there were any shrewdness in him, he must have set it down by this time as a special trait in me.

"Well, anyhow you understand the 'Fair Maid of Perth,'" added he.

"Yes," answered I. "The heroine is like my sister, — beautiful, and dreadfully good."

I was ashamed directly I had said it : praising one's sister was almost like praising one's self.

"Indeed," said he. "That's not a fault from which most of us suffer ; but then very few of us have people at hand ready and generous enough to sing our praises."

I might have taken the speech as a compliment, I suppose ; but it seemed so natural to praise Joyce, that I confess it rather puzzled me.

"You must miss your sister," added Mr Harrod.

"Of course I do," cried I, warmly.

" Luckily she isn't going to be away for long, or I don't know what mother would do.   She's mother's right hand in the house. I'm no use indoors."

" You always seem to me to be very busy," said Harrod.

" Oh no," insisted I ; " it was father I used to help."

" Don't you help him now ? " asked he.

" No," I answered shortly ; and as I spoke the recollection of my grievance swept over me, and brought the tears very close,—" he doesn't need me."

Mr Harrod did not say a word, he did not even look at me, and I was grateful to him for that ; but I was sure that he had understood, and I grew more sore than ever, knowing that I had let him guess at my tender place.   We walked on in silence.

" I   used   to   love   the   Waverley   novels when I was a lad," said he, changing the subject kindly.

" Don't you now ? " asked I.

" I daresay I should if I read them, but I have to read stiffer books now — when I read at all."

" Books on agriculture, I suppose!" said I,
scornfully. " But father says a little practical knowledge is worth all the books in the
world."

It did not strike me at the moment how
very rude this speech was; but Mr Harrod
smiled.

" Your father is quite right, Miss Maliphant," said he. " Books are of little use
till tested by practical knowledge; but after
all, if they are good books, they were written
from practical knowledge, you know, and
perhaps it would take one a lifetime to reap
the individual knowledge of all that they
have swept together."

" I only know what father said," repeated
I, half sullenly.

" Perhaps you don't remember it all," said
he. " I think your father would agree with
me there; he is a very wise man, and I fancy
I have stated the case pretty fairly."

" I should think he *was* a wise man!" I
exclaimed, and I think my pride was pardonable this time. " All the country-side knows
that."

"I know it," he answered. " One can't go

into a cottage without hearing him spoken of with love and reverence."

"Yes; I never saw any one so sorry for people as father is," answered I. "I'm frightened of people who are ill and un-happy; but father, he wants to help them—well, just as I want to help the beasts and birds," I ended up with a laugh.

As I spoke the curious twittering note of the female cuckoo sounded in one of the trees upon the cliff, and immediately from four different quarters, one after the other, the reply came in the two distinct notes of the male bird. I stood still upon the path, and looked about me. The sound, and per-haps partly what I had just said, reminded me of one of the objects of my walk.

"I declare I had almost forgotten," I cried, and without another word of explanation I dashed up the bank of the cliff, Taff fol-lowing.

Mr Harrod stood below on the path. A few minutes more were enough to enable me to find the bush, which I had marked with a bit of the braid off my cloak on that memor-able evening a few nights ago.

The lark's nest was still there. The cruel little cuckoo sat in it alone, while hovering in the air, close at hand, was the foolish mother, waiting, with a dainty morsel in her beak, till I should be gone, and she could safely feed the vicious little interloper who had destroyed her own brood. The bodies of the little titlarks lay upon the bank. I jumped down to the path again and told Mr Harrod the tale.

" I wish I had put the cuckoo out," I said. " I hate cuckoos—all the more because every one admires them." And I remember that all the way home I kept reverting to that distressing little piece of bird-tragedy.

We returned by the sea-shore. It was a longer way, but I declared that I must have a sight of the ocean on this soft, calm day. And soft it was, and calm and grey and mild. The sun was setting, but there was no sunset. Only behind the village on the hill the clouds lifted a little towards the horizon, and left a line of whiter light, against which the trees and houses detached themselves vividly ; the marsh was uniform and sober.

When we had climbed the steep road and

were at the Grange gates, Mr Harrod held
out his hand and said, as he bade me good
night, " I don't see why you shouldn't be of
just as much use to your father as ever you
were, Miss Maliphant.   Please, be very sure
that no one ever would or ever could replace
you to your father."

He spoke as though it were not altogether
easy for him to do so ; but there was a ring
of honest kindliness in his voice that left me
mute, and almost ashamed.   He held my
hand a moment in his strong grip, but he did
not look at me ; and then he turned and
almost fled down the road, as if he, too, were
almost ashamed of what he had said.

And I had not answered a word.   I stood
there surprised, perplexed, and even a little
frightened, surrounded by new and curious
emotions, which I did not even try to unravel.

CHAPTER XVII.

I DO not suppose that I had the dimmest notion at the time that this man, whom I considered my foe, had sprung surely, and as soon as I saw him, into that mysterious blank space that exists in every woman's imagination, waiting to be filled by the figure that shall henceforth bound her horizon. I do not suppose that I guessed at my real feelings for a moment. If I had done so, I am sure that it would only have aggravated my hostile attitude, whereas my first most unreasonable mood was beginning slowly to lapse into one of friendly interest, and of eager desire to be of use.

It is poor sport keeping up an attitude of defiance towards a person who is entirely unconscious of one's intention ; and whether Mr Harrod was really unconscious of my intention or not, he certainly acted as if he were, and was, as far as his reserved nature would allow, so friendly towards me, that I could not choose but be friendly towards him in return. Anyhow, it is true that ere three weeks had passed, that began to happen which Joyce had so anxiously desired : Mr Harrod and I began to make friends over our common interests.

A certain amount of defiance had begun to be transferred in me from him, whose coming I had so bitterly resented, to those who shared that resentment of mine.

Reuben was still sadly refractory. Luckily he was not much among the men ; but where there's a will there's a way, and I'm afraid he had influence enough to do no good. And Deborah troubled me more. Although mother was for the bailiff, because he was the Squire's friend, and also because, I think, she was really far more anxious about father's health than she allowed us to guess, and wanted him to be saved work—Deborah had not really allowed herself to be convinced, as she generally was.

She was not unreasonable ; she was too

clever to be unreasonable, and she loved us all too dearly to resent any step which she chose to believe was for the good of any of us. But I am sure she never believed that this step was for the good of any of us. From beginning to end she never liked Trayton Harrod. And what specially annoyed me about her at this time was, that she pretended to be trying to make me like him; and as I innocently began to change my own feelings, so I naturally began to resent this attitude in her.

On the very afternoon of which I am thinking, I resented Deborah's attitude. I had been in the kitchen making cakes (when Joyce was away, it was I who had to make the cakes), and Deborah had taken advantage of the opportunity to follow up the line already begun by my sister, and to beg me, for father's sake, to forget my grievance and to be gracious to the young bailiff. As may be imagined, Deborah did not think that she was bound to show any consideration in the matter of what she said to us girls.

" I know it comes hard on you, my dear,"

said she. "There's lots of little jobs you used to do afore, and no doubt did just as well, that'll be this young man's place to do now, and he won't notice whether you mind it or no. 'Tain't likely. But so long as he don't interfere with what we've got to do, we'll mind our own business and never give him a thought. You see, child, it's your father has got to say whether the young man's a-helping or a-hindering. Maybe he'll find out these chaps, that have learnt it all on book and paper, don't know the top from the bottom any better nor he do himself. But that's for them to settle atween 'em, and it's none of our look-out."

I don't know why this speech should specially have irritated me, but it did. Even if I had begun to guess that I was growing to like Mr Harrod better than I had intended to like him, I certainly should not have been glad that any one else should guess it. But the fact is, that I believe I had lived the last fortnight without any thought, and that this speech of Deborah's roused me to an investigation of my feelings which was annoying to me.

"I have no intention at all of being rude, Deb," exclaimed I. "I leave that to you. I don't think it's lady-like to be rude."

Deb laughed.

"Oh, come now, none of your hoighty-toightyness!" exclaimed she. "Who carried on up-stairs and down when first Squire talked about a bailiff to master at all? I haven't nursed you when you were a baby not to know when you're in a bad temper. It's plain enough, my dear."

"I know I have a bad temper," said I; "but I don't see that that has anything to do with the matter."

I suppose something in the way I said it must have touched old Deb, who had a soft heart for all her rough ways, for she said in her topsy-turvy way—

"Well, there—no more I don't see that it has. All I mean is, that if you let him alone he'll let you alone, and no harm done. You'll have the more time for your books, and for looking after your clothes a bit. You know I've often told you you'll never get a beau so long as you go about gipsying as you do."

" Deborah, how dare you ! " cried I, angrily.
" You know very well that——"

"That I wouldn't have a lover for anything in the world," I was going to say, and
deeply perjure myself; but at that very moment mother opened the door and looked
into the kitchen. She had her spectacles
still on her nose, and an open letter in her
hand.

"Margaret, I want you," said she, shortly,
"in the parlour."

" I can't come just now, mother," answered
I. " The cakes will burn."

"Deborah will see to the cakes," said
mother, and I knew by her voice that I
must do as she bade me. "I want you at
once."

I knew what it was about. Two days ago
I had had a letter from Joyce. It gave me
no news : she had got on with her tapestry ;
she had trimmed herself a new bonnet ; Aunt
Naomi's rheumatism was no better ; she
hoped that father's gout had not returned,
—no news until the very end. Then she
said she had been to the Royal Academy
of pictures in London, with an old lady who

lived close to Aunt Naomi, and that she had there met Captain Forrester.

Certainly this was a big enough piece of news to suffice for one letter. But why had Joyce put it at the very end? and why did she hurry it over as quickly as possible, making no sort or kind of comment upon it? It was another of the things about Joyce that I could not make out. Why was she not proud of her engagement? Why did she never care to speak of it? I thought that if I were engaged to a man whom I loved, I should be very proud of it, whereas she always seemed anxious to avoid the subject.

Of course it was horrible to be parted from him, but then it should lighten her burden to speak of it to some one who sympathised with her as I did. But I knew well enough why it was. It all came from that over-strained notion of duty. She had promised mother that she would not see Frank, and would not write to Frank, and would not speak of Frank, and she kept so strictly to the letter of this promise that she would not speak of him even to me.

When first I had read Joyce's letter, I had

been angry with her for a cold-hearted girl,
but now I was not angry with her. I admired her, but I made up my mind that
her passion for self-sacrifice should not wreck
her life's happiness if I could prevent it.
Face to face it was difficult to scold Joyce.
There was a kind of gentle obstinacy about
her which took one unawares, and was very
hard to deal with. But in a letter I could
speak my mind, and I would speak my mind
—not only to her, but, what was far more
difficult, to mother also. So that when
mother put her head in at the kitchen-door
and summoned me to the parlour, I guessed
what it was about, and I knew pretty well
what I was going to say. She put the letter
into my hand and sat down, looking up at
me over her spectacles as I read it, with her
clear blue eyes intent and a little frown on
her white brow. It was from Aunt Naomi,
and it said that a young man named Captain
Forrester had just been to call upon Joyce:
she thought she noticed a certain confusion on Joyce's part during his presence;
she therefore wrote at once to know
whether his visits were sanctioned by her

parents, as she did not wish to get into any trouble.

Oh, what a horrid old woman she was! How could people be narrow-minded and selfish to such a point as that, I said to myself. Mother watched me, and Deborah came into the room to lay the cloth. It was just curiosity that brought her.

" It's a ridiculous letter," said I roughly, throwing it down with an ill grace, and looking defiantly, not at mother, but at the old woman, who regarded me with reproving eyes. " Why in the world shouldn't Joyce receive a visit from a gentleman—still more from the man she's going to marry ? "

" She's not going to marry him—at least, not with my free consent," said mother, putting her lips together in a set curve that I knew.

" Well, then, of course it will be a great pity, but I suppose it will have to be without your consent," said I rashly.

" Well, I'm sure," ejaculated Deborah under her breath, and looking at me with something like remonstrance. Mother rose with dignity, and turning to the table she

said, " Deborah, would you be so kind as to
fetch in the cold ham ? "

Of course Deborah knew that she was
being sent out of the room that I might have
a piece of mother's mind, and my own was
a struggle between pleasure that Deborah
should for once be set down, and anger that
she should know the reason of her dismissal.
She stayed a moment, setting the forks round
the table to a nicety of precision ; then, as
she passed out of the room, she gave me a
friendly nudge, and looked at me a moment
with a sort of humorous kindliness in her
shrewd grey eyes.

Mother took up the letter again. " Do
you know how Captain Forrester learnt where
Joyce was staying ? " asked she.

" No ; how should I know ? " answered I.
" Joyce told me that she had met him acci-
dentally at the Royal Academy. I suppose
he found out where she was. Where there's
a will there's a way."

" But he undertook not to try and see
her," remarked mother severely. " His conduct is dishonourable."

" Well, you might make some allowances,"

cried I. "It shows he loves her; it shows she will be happy with him. And look here, mother," added I, in a sudden frenzy of frankness,—"I believe that if I were to get the chance of doing anything to help to bring them together, I should do it."

Mother looked at me fixedly. "No, you wouldn't," said she at last. "You're head-strong and mistaken, but you're honest. You've taken your word you wouldn't inter-fere nor mention the matter to any one for a year, and you'll keep your word."

I knew very well that she was right, but I said boldly, "Joyce is my sister; I love her, I want her to be happy, and I shall do what I can to make her so."

Still mother looked at me. "You forget that I want Joyce to be happy too," said she. "If she is your sister, she is also my daughter." There was a tremble in her voice, whether of anger or distress I did not know.

"Of course I know very well that you care about her and her happiness," said I; "but perhaps you don't see what is best for it. How can old people, whose youth is past ever so long ago, remember how young

people feel ?   They can't know what young
folk need to be happy as well as others of
their own age can."

" Maybe they can look ahead a bit better,
though," said mother, without deigning to
argue with me.   " Be that as it may, I don't
think I'll ask you to teach me what's best for
my children's happiness.   I may be all wrong,
of course, but I mean to try and have my own
way as long as I can, though I know very
well we can't expect the duty and reverence
we used to pay our parents when I was your
age."

I felt that the rebuke was deserved, and I
was silent.

" At all events, it's no business of yours,"
continued mother.   " If the thing has got to
be fought out, I would rather fight it out
with Joyce herself.   If she insists upon marrying the young man, I suppose she can do
so.   She is of age."

I did not answer her, but I laughed.   The
idea of Joyce insisting upon doing anything
was too ridiculous.   And, of course, mother
knew this quite well, so that it was not quite
fair of her.

Having once begun to laugh, the spell of my ill-humour was, however, broken, and it was in a very different tone of voice that I said, " Come, mother, you know very well that sister is far too gentle, and loves you far too much, ever to do anything against your wish—so that's ridiculous, isn't it ? "

Mother smiled. " Yes, yes, she's a good girl," she said. " You are both of you good children, but you mustn't be so self-sufficient and headstrong."

" Well, I suppose I am headstrong," said I ; " I'm sorry for it. But Joyce isn't. I do think she ought to be put upon less than folk who are. I believe if nobody fought Joyce's battles, she'd let herself be wiped right out."

And, sure enough, by the afternoon post there came a letter from Joyce which satisfied mother more than it did me. It explained that Captain Forrester had come to Sydenham uninvited and unwelcome ; and it begged mother to believe that he would never come again.

CHAPTER XVIII.

THURSDAY was the day for making the butter,
and one Thursday, in the beginning of June
of the year I am recording, I walked along
the flagstones of the courtyard towards the
dairy, that stood somewhat detached from
the house. I hummed softly to myself as I
went; I was happy. I could not have told
why I was happy—for Joyce was away, and
I should have been lonely. But the June
was fair and pleasant, and I was young and
strong.

Mother had a special pride in her dairy.
The broad low pans stood in their order
on the dressers along the white-tiled walls,
each of the four "meals" in its place; the
household cream set apart, and other clean
pans ready for the fresh setting. The warm
summer breeze came through the trellised

shutters that let the air in day and night, and through the open door, around which the midsummer roses clustered thickly, and the honeysuckle twined its sweet tendrils.

Beyond the door one could see the square of grass-plot, with the wide border running round it, in which old-fashioned flowers stood up against the brick wall; and over the wall one could see just a little strip of marsh and sea in the distance. Mother had not come in yet; but Reuben had churned before day-break, and now Deborah stood lifting the butter out of the churn, ready for the washing and pressing.

"Have you seen Reuben anywheres about?" said she sharply, as I came in.

I knew by her voice that she was annoyed.

"Yes," said I; "I've just left him. Do you want him?"

"I want a few faggots for my kitchen fire; but nowadays there's no getting no one to do nothing," answered she. "Reuben was never much for brains, but he used to be handy; but now — if there's nothing, there's always something for Reuben to do."

"Dear me! How's that?" asked I.

Deborah was silent. She had said already far more than was her wont—for Deborah was not one to talk, and generally kept her grievances to herself.

"The butter 'll want a deal o' pressing and washing this morning," said she. "The weather's sultry, and it hasn't come clean."

I was turning up my sleeves. "Dear me! Then it'll take a long time?" said I. I hated washing the butter,—it was dull work.

"Sure enough it will," laughed Deborah grimly. "What do you want to be doing? You haven't half the heart in the work that your sister has!"

"Ah no," I agreed. "I'm not so clever at it as Joyce is."

"You can be clever enough when you choose," said the old woman sagely. "I daresay you could be clever enough teaching this Mr Harrod his way about the farm if you were wanted to."

I looked up quickly. I think I blushed. Why did Deb say that? But why should I blush because she had said it?

"Indeed I shouldn't think of trying to teach Mr Harrod anything," said I, attempting to laugh.

"What! Has he turned out sharp enough to please you after all?" asked she, with that peculiar snort which it was her fashion to give when she wanted to be disagreeable. "I thought you were of a mind that nobody could be clever enough over this precious farm, unless you was to show them how."

"Fiddlesticks!" said I.

It was very annoying of Deborah to want to put me in a bad temper when I had come in in such a good one.

"Have you seen your father?" asked she presently.

"No," replied I. "Does he want me?"

"He was asking for you. Wanted you to go up and show this young chap the field where he wants the turnips put."

The bailiff again. What was the matter with Deborah, that she could not leave me and him alone?

"Mr Harrod knows his way about the country quite well enough by this time to find it for himself," I said.

I did not look at Deborah, but I knew
very well that her face wore a kind of expression of defiant mischief with which I was
familiar.

"I'm sorry you're still set again the poor
young man," said she provokingly.

But there was a very different ring in her
voice when she spoke again in a few minutes,
and when I looked up I saw that an unwonted gentleness had overspread her hard
rough features.

"If you haven't seen your father since
breakfast," she added, "maybe you don't
know as he's had another o' them queer
starts at his heart."

"No. What kind of thing?" asked I,
frightened.

"Oh, you know; same as he had in
the winter, only not so bad. There, you
needn't be terrified," added she; "it's nothing bad much—only lasted a minute or two.
He called and asked me for a glass of
water, and I fetched the missus. He was
better afore she came. But it's my belief
he's neither so young nor so well as he
was."

This was evident; but neither Deb nor I saw the joke—we were too serious.

"And it's my belief he's fretting over something, Margaret," added she gravely. "So if this here new chap saves him any bother, I suppose folk should need be pleased."

I wondered whether Deborah meant this as an excuse for my being pleased, or as a rebuke for my not being pleased. I think now that she meant it as neither, but rather as a rebuke to herself. I took it to heart, however, and the tears rushed to my eyes.

Had I been really anxious to save father all possible worry over this innovation? Had I done all I could to help Mr Harrod settle down in his place? I was not sure. I thought I would do more, and yet I thought I would not do more. O Margaret, Margaret! were you quite honest with yourself at that time? I took up a fresh lump of butter, and began washing it blindly.

"Come, come, you're not going the right way about! You'll never get the milk out that way!" cried Deborah, coming up to me.

"No, no—I know," answered I impatiently; and then, incoherently, " but, oh dear me! what is the right way?"

Deborah laughed, but gently enough. She was a clever old woman, and she knew that I was not alluding to the butter.

"Well, I don't rightly know myself," said she, without looking at me. "What you thinks the right way, most times turns out to be the wrong way; and when you make folk turn to the right when they was minded to turn to the left, it's most like the left would ha' been the best way for them to travel after all. I've done advisin' long ago; for it's a queer tract of country here below, and every one has to take their own chance in the long-run."

This speech of Deb's had given me time to choke down my ridiculous tears and put on my usual face again, for I should indeed have been ashamed to be caught crying when there was nothing in the world to cry about; and just as she finished speaking, mother's figure came past the window, walking slowly, Squire Broderick at her side.

"Oh dear me, whatever does Squire want at this time o' day!" cried I impatiently.

"He shouldn't need to come so often, now Joyce is away."

Deborah looked at me warningly. The latticed shutters, although they looked closed, let in every sound; and indeed I don't know what possessed me to make the speech, for I had no dislike to the Squire. I suppose I was still a little ruffled.

"You might keep a civil tongue in your head!" grumbled Deborah angrily.

The Squire was, I have said, a great favourite with the old woman, who was, so to speak, on the Tory side of the camp, although she would have been puzzled to explain the meaning of the word.

Mother was talking to the Squire in her most doleful voice—a voice that she could produce at times, although she was certainly not by nature a doleful woman.

"It has upset me very much," she was saying, and I knew she was alluding to father's indisposition. "He says it is only rheumatics, and I hope it is; but it makes me uneasy. He's not the man he was, and I can't help fancying at times that he has something on his mind that worries him."

The very same words that Deborah had used; but what father should have specially to worry him, I could not see.

"He gives too much thought to these high-flown notions of his, Mrs Maliphant—that's what it is," answered the Squire testily. "It's enough to turn any man's brain."

"Oh, I don't think it's that. I think it cheers him up to think of the misery of the working classes," declared mother simply, without any notion of the contradiction of her speech. "I'm sure he's quite happy when he gets a letter from your nephew about the meetings over this children's institution. It's a notion of his own, you see, and he's pleased with it, as we all are with what we have fancied out. Not but what I do say it is a beautiful notion," added mother loyally. "I pity the poor little things myself—no one more."

This was true. It was the only one of father's "wild notions" that mother had any touch of.

I noticed that the Squire had frowned at the mention of Frank's name. He always did,—I thought I knew why.

" Yes ; that's all very fine, ma'am," he said, " but the trouble is that it won't make his crops grow. No; and paying his labourers half as much again as anybody else won't make his farm pay."

Mother looked at the Squire anxiously.

"Do you think the farm doesn't pay?" asked she. "Do you suppose it's that as is making Laban fidgety?"

"How should I know, my dear lady?" answered the Squire in the same irritable way—he was very irritable this morning—" Maliphant knows his own affairs."

Mother was silent.

" Well, I hope this young fellow is going to do a deal o' good to the farm, and to my husband too," added she cheerfully. "I look to a great deal from him, and I can't be grateful enough to you, Squire Broderick, for having settled the matter for us. He's a plain-speaking, sensible young man, and I like him very much."

" Yes, Harrod is a thorough good fellow," answered the Squire warmly. " He *is* plain-speaking—too much so to his elders sometimes ; but it's because he has got his whole heart in his work. He cares for nothing else, and you can't say that of every man that works for another man's money."

They had stopped outside the window, and had stood still there, talking all this while. I suppose mother forgot that Deb and I were bound to be inside doing our business, and that the lattice was open.

" I like him very much," continued she; " but I don't think Laban fancies him much, nor yet Margaret. Margaret set her face against his coming from the first, you see. It was natural, I daresay. She had been used to do a good bit for her father, and when Margaret sets her face against any-thing—well, you can't lead her, it's driving then. It's just the same when she wants a thing. You may drive and drive, but you won't drive her away from that spot. It's very hard to know how to manage a nature like that, Mr Broderick, especially when you've been used to a girl that's as gentle as Joyce is. But there, they both have their goods and their ills. Far be it from their mother to deny that."

Squire Broderick laughed, and then mother

laughed too, and they both came forward
round the corner and in at the door. Mother
started a little when she saw me, and the
Squire smiled curiously. But I did not
smile; I was boiling over with anger.

"Why, Deborah, you have set to work
early," said mother, without looking at me.
"Why didn't you call me?"

"I didn't know as there was any need to
call," answered Deborah roughly, and I believe in my heart that she was the more
rough because she didn't like mother's speech
about me. "You've your work to do, ma'am,
and I've mine. I suppose as you'd come
when you wanted to, but that was no reason
why Margaret and I should wait about,
twirling our thumbs."

Mother did not reply. I felt the Squire's
gaze still upon me, and I looked up and gave
him a bold, angry glance. I am sure that
my eyes must have flashed, and I think that
my lips were set in the hard lines that mother
used to tell me made me look so ugly. I
hated the Squire to look at me, and he
seemed to guess it, for he turned away at
once, and afterwards I remembered how he

had done it, and that somehow his face had looked almost tender.

But mother did not seem to care a bit that I should have overheard what she said : she began turning up the skirt of her soft grey gown and rolling up her sleeves. Mother always wore grey when she did not wear the old black satin brocade that had belonged to her own mother, and which only came out on high days and holy days. She had said she would never put on colours again, when our little brother died many years ago ; and I am glad she never did, for I should not like to remember her in anything but the soft tones that became her so well. Black, grey, or white—she never wore anything else.

"The dairy is not what it is when Joyce is at home," said she, deprecatingly, to the Squire.

"Well, to be sure, ma'am, I don't see what's amiss with it," declared Deborah. "It's hard as them as go away idling should be put above them as stay at home and work."

I looked at Deborah in surprise. She was not wont to set Joyce down.

"Why, the place looks as if you could eat off the floor,—what more do you want, Mrs Maliphant?" laughed the Squire, coming up and standing beside me. "And I'm sure nobody could make up a pat better than Miss Margaret."

"Margaret has been more used to out-door work," said mother, at which Deb gave one of her snorts, I did not know why, except out of pure contradiction, for she had blamed my butter-making herself five minutes before.

"You seem to have plenty of cream," said the Squire, walking round.

"Yes," answered mother; "our cows are doing well now, though Daisy will give richer cream to her pail than all the rest put together." Then she added, without looking at me, "Margaret, you need not do any more just now. Your father was asking for you. Go to him, and come back when he has done with you."

I wiped my arms silently, and turned down my sleeves. I had not said a single word since she had come in. She looked at me, but I would not return her glance. I

was a wrong-headed, foolish girl, and when
I thought that mother had been unjust to
me, I tried to make her suffer for it.

I walked straight out of the dairy without a word to any one, and it was not till I
was outside that I saw that the Squire had
followed me. He was talking to me, so I
had to listen to him.

" Yes," I said vaguely, in answer to him,
—for of course the remark, although I had
not entirely caught it, had been about my
sister,—"yes, Joyce is very well; but she
is not coming back just yet. I don't want
her to come back just yet. I think it's so
good for her to be away. When she is at
home, mother wants her every minute. It
isn't always to do something, but it's always
to be there. And Joyce is good. She always seems pleased to have no free life of
her own. But she can't really *be* pleased. *I*
couldn't. Anyhow it can't be good for her to
be so dreadfully unselfish, do you think so ? "

In my eagerness I was actually taking the
Squire into my confidence. He smiled.

" Miss Joyce always appeared to me to be
very contented, doing the things about the

house that your mother wished," said he. "You mustn't judge every one by yourself. People generally try to get something of what they want, I fancy. You're sister isn't so independent as you are."

"No," agreed I, gloomily, "she isn't. She's what folk call more womanly. I never was intended for a woman. Father always says I ought to have been a boy."

"I don't think women are all unwomanly because they're independent," said the Squire. And then he added, in a lower voice, "I don't think you're unwomanly."

We had come round by the lawn, and we stood there a moment before the porch. The bees were busy among the summer flowers, and the scent of roses and mignonette, of sweet-peas and heliotrope, was heavy upon the air. The sun streamed down on our heads, and upon the green marsh beneath the cliff, and upon the sea in the distance. It was a bright, hot June day. I was just going indoors, when the Squire laid his hand on my arm.

"Wait a minute, Miss Margaret, I want to say something to you," he said.

I looked at him surprised. Was he going
to ask me to intercede with Joyce for him?
If so, he had come very decidedly to the
wrong person. But something in his face
made me look away.

"I won't keep you long," said he.

And then he paused, while I waited with
my face turned aside.

"I don't think you'll take what I'm going
to say amiss, Miss Margaret," he went on at
last. "I've known you such a long time—
ever since you were a little girl—that I don't
feel as though I were taking a liberty, as I
should if you were a stranger. I don't suppose you remember how I used to help you
scramble out of the dykes when you got a
ducking on the marsh after the rainfalls, and
how I used to take you into the house-
keeper's room at the Manor to have your
frock dried, so that you should not get into
a scrape? But *I* remember it very well, and
the cakes that you used to love with the
blackberry jam in them, and the rides that
you used to have on my back after the
school feasts."

He paused a moment, as though for an

answer. I gave him none, but I remembered all that he alluded to very well.

"You don't mind my speaking, do you?" repeated he again.

"Oh no, I don't mind," answered I, with a little laugh.

"Having known you like that all your life, I care for you so much," continued he, "that I can't bear to see you doing yourself an injustice."

I looked at him now straight. I felt annoyed, after all, at what I knew he was going to say. But the kindness and gentleness of his face disarmed me.

"You mean that I don't behave well to my mother," said I, the flush of sudden vexation dying away from my face. "Mother doesn't understand me. I can't always be of the same mind as she is. I don't see why people need always be of the same mind as their relations; but it doesn't follow that they're ungrateful and heartless because they are not. I've heard mother say that she doesn't believe that I care any more for her than for any tramp upon the high-road. But that isn't true."

The Squire laughed.

"No; of course it isn't true," said he, "and Mrs Maliphant doesn't think it."

"Oh yes, I think she does sometimes," persisted I. "She would like me to be like Joyce. But I shall never be like Joyce!"

"No," assented the Squire, decidedly, "I don't think you ever will be. But it was not specially with reference to your mother that I was going to speak to you, although what I was going to say bears, I fancy, on what vexed her to-day."

I bit my lip. Was he going to refer to Mr Harrod? He paused again.

"Your father is very much harassed and troubled, I fear, Miss Margaret," he said next. "I have noticed with much grief, of late, how sadly he seems to have aged."

"Do you think so?" said I. "I don't know what he should have to be harassed about."

"The conduct of a farm is a very harassing thing: it takes all a man's thought and care. And even then it doesn't always pay," said the Squire gravely.

I did not answer; I was puzzled.

"Your father is getting old," continued he, "and it is hard for a man, when he is old, to give as much attention to such things as in youth and strength."

"I don't think he is so very old," I said, half vexed; "but perhaps he doesn't care so much about farming as some people do. Perhaps he cares more about other things."

"Perhaps," said the Squire evasively. Then starting off afresh, he added quickly, "I had hoped that this new bailiff would have relieved him of some anxiety; but I am afraid there are inconveniences connected with his presence which, to a man of your father's temperament, are particularly galling."

"Well, I suppose it's natural that a man who has been his own master all his life should mind taking a younger one's advice," said I, pretty hotly this time.

"Of course it is," agreed the Squire; "but all the same, the farm needs a younger man's head and a younger man's heart in it before it'll thrive as it ought. And now I'm coming to what I wanted to say, Miss Margaret.

You can do more than any one else to
smooth over the difficulties. You must persuade your father to let Harrod have his
own way. He's a headstrong chap, I can
see that; and he'll do nothing, he'll take
no interest, if he's gainsaid at every step.
Nobody would. There are many kinds of
modern improvements that are needed at
Knellestone. Your father has always stood
against them, because he fancied it wasn't
fair to the labourers; but they'll have to
come, and I know very well Harrod won't
stay here long and not get them. No man
who is honest to his employer would. Now,
you must be go-between," he went on, still
more earnestly, although speaking in a low
voice. "You must get your father to see
things reasonably, and you must be friendly
to Harrod : show him that you take an interest in his improvements, and persuade
him that your father does also. So he will,
when he sees how they work. I can see
that a vast deal depends upon you, Miss
Margaret. You're a clever girl; you can
manage it—*if you will.*"

I turned my face further aside than ever;

—in fact, I think I turned my back. I did not answer—I did not know what to answer.

"And you *will*, I know," added he, in a persuasive voice. "I quite understand that it isn't pleasant to you at first, but it will become so when you see that *you* can do a great deal to make things smooth when difficulties occur. I am sure it must be a great comfort to you to think of how much there still is in which you can help your father,—quite as much as there used to be in the past, when you had it more your own way. No one else can help him as you can help him."

"Oh, I don't really think he wants help," said I, but rather by way of saying something than from conviction.

"Well, I think he wants more than you fancy," persisted the Squire. "I would not for worlds cast a shadow over your young life, Miss Margaret!" he went on earnestly; "but I feel that it is the part of a true friend that I should, in a certain measure, do so. Your mother is a tender helpmeet and an admirable nurse, I know; but there are other things needed for a man besides physic and poultices.   The time may come when he may turn to you for some things, and I think you should make yourself ready for that time."

He said no more.   But after a few moments he held out his hand.

"Good-bye," said he.   "Whenever you want a friend, I don't need to tell you that you have got one at the Manor."

He was gone, and I had stood there with downcast head, and had answered never a word.   I did not at the time understand all that he had said, nor what he had meant by his doubts and his fears, although in after years his words came back to me very vividly, as did also other words of Deborah's; but one thing was very clear to me even then, and that was that everybody — from Joyce and Deborah to mother and the Squire — considered that I ought to make friends with the new bailiff, and that I had had not yet done so sufficiently.

CHAPTER XIX.

FROM that time forth I gave myself up un-
reservedly to following the Squire's advice. Yes, I did not even shrink from any
possible charge of inconsistency. Deborah
might laugh at me if she liked, Reuben
might look askance out of his stolid
silence, mother might ponder; but I had
been convinced. I knew what I had to
do, and I would stand Trayton Harrod's
friend. That was what I argued to myself. Was I quite honest? At all events
I was very happy.

One morning—it must have been about a
week after the Squire's words to me—I had
occasion to go out on to our cliff to plant out
some cuttings that Joyce had procured and
sent me from London. Reuben was in the
orchard hard by, mowing the grass under the

apple-trees. He did such work when hands were few. The orchard was only divided by a wall from the garden, and Reuben and I kept up a brisk conversation across it.

"I've heeard say as Mister Harrod be for persuading master to have new sorts o' hops planted along the hillside this year, miss," Reuben was saying."

"Indeed," said I. "Well, I suppose ours aren't a good sort, then?"

"That's for them as knows to say," replied the old man. "The Lord have made growths for every part, and it's ill flyin' in the face of the Lord."

"Well, Mr Harrod knows," declared I.

"Nay, miss, he warn't born and bred hereabouts. But I says to him, 'You ask Jack Barnstaple,' says I. 'He knows,' says I."

"You said that to Mr Harrod, Reuben!" I exclaimed.

"Yes, miss," he answered. "I did."

"Well, then, I think it was very rude of you, Reuben. That's all I have to say."

"Nay, miss, I heeard you say as how a stranger wouldn't be o' no good to master," grinned Reuben. "They don't understand."

" If I said that, I made a great mistake,"
answered I half angrily. " I think Mr Harrod is a great deal of use."

"Well, miss, if he be a-going to have
Goldings planted in instead of Early Prolifics, he won't get no change out o' the
ground, that's what I say. They won't
thrive for nobody, and they won't do it to
please him."

Reuben shouldered his scythe as he said
the last words, and went off to a more distant part of the orchard, and I set to work
at my planting. I knew pretty well by this
time that it was worse than waste of time
taking Mr Harrod's side against Reuben.

I wondered what he would have thought
if he could have heard me taking his side.
But I don't think he thought much about
having a "side." He was too eager about
his work.

I set to planting my cuttings busily—so
busily that I did not hear steps on the gravel
behind me, and looked up suddenly to see Mr
Harrod on the path beside me. He did not
say anything, but stood a while watching me.
At last I stood up with the trowel in my

hand, and my face, I do not doubt, very red and hot beneath my big print sun-bonnet.

"Did you meet Reuben just now?" asked I, rather by way of saying something.

"No," answered he; "I've come straight from your father's room. He wants you."

"Does he? Well, I can't go this minute. I must finish this job. I've neglected it for a week. What does he want me for?"

I knelt down and began my work again.

"He and I have been discussing a new scheme," said Mr Harrod, without answering my question.

"What! about co-operation and children's schools and things!" cried I with a smile. "Is he going to press you into it too?"

"Oh no; about the farm," answered he. "His possessions in hops are very small, and there's a fine and unusual chance just turned up of making money. I want him to take on another small farm—specially for hops."

"To take on another farm!" repeated I.

"Yes," said he; "but he doesn't take to it. I think he must have something else in his head. But the matter must be decided at once, for I hear there's another man after it."

"Where is it?" I asked, a secret glow of satisfaction in my heart to think he should come and tell me of this as he did.

"It's 'The Elms,'" he answered, "below the mill on the slope yonder."

I stood up and stopped my gardening to show I took an interest in what he was saying. "I know 'The Elms' well enough," I said, "but I didn't know it was to let."

"Yes," he replied. "Old Searle left his affairs in a dreadful mess when he died, and the executors have decided to sell the crops at a valuation, and let the place at once without waiting till the usual term."

"Dear me! what an odd thing," said I. "I thought farms were never let excepting at Michaelmas."

"Never is a long word," smiled Mr Harrod. "It is unusual. But I suppose the executors don't care for the expense of putting in a bailiff till October. Anyhow, they appear to want to realise at once; and it's a good chance for us."

"It's all hop-gardens at 'The Elms,' isn't it?" asked I.

"Yes; chief part."

"It seems to me it must either be a very poor crop, or they must want a good price for it so late in the season," said I, not ill-pleased with myself for what I considered the rare shrewdness of this remark.

But Mr Harrod smiled again. "The price will be the average of what the crops fetched during the past three years," said he. "That's law now. I should say about £36 to the acre. Leastways, that would be the price ready for picking, but there'll be a reduction at this time of year. That'll be a matter for private bargain."

"Yes," said I. "There'll be many a risk between now and picking."

"Of course," said the bailiff, half testily. "But it's just about the best-looking crop in these parts at the present time. They *will* plant those Early Prolifics about here. I suppose it's because they can get them sooner into the market. But they're a poor hop. Now the plants at 'The Elms' are all Goldings or Jones."

"But they say the Goldings will never thrive in our soil," said I.

" *They ;* who are *they ?* " retorted Harrod. " They know nothing about it."

" No, I daresay you're right," I hastened to say. " Only hops are always considered risky, aren't they?"

" Everything is risky," answered he more gently. " But as I have an interest in selling the crop to advantage if it turns out well, I don't believe your father could go very far wrong over it."

"Well, if you think it would be such a safe speculation, of course father ought to be persuaded to go in for it," said I.

" I really think so," answered Harrod confidently.

" But perhaps he doesn't think he can afford the rent of it," suggested I after a pause ; " perhaps he hasn't the ready money."

" I can scarcely believe that, Miss Maliphant. Your father passes for a rich man in the county," answered he with a smile. " No ; he thinks the property is good enough as it has stood all these years.   But, as a matter of fact, it would be a far more valuable one if it had better hop-gardens.   Hops are the staple produce of the county, and I am sorry to say he doesn't stand as well in that line as many of the farmers about : he wants some one to give him courage to make this venture.   Unluckily he has not confidence enough in me, and Squire Broderick is away in London."

"Is the Squire away ?" asked I.

"Yes; I have just inquired, by your father's wish."

"I'll go and talk to father," said I with youthful self-confidence, gathering up my tools, and too happy in feeling that I was the supporter of the man who, but a fortnight ago, I had sworn to treat as an open enemy, to be troubled by any misgivings.

As I might have known, I did not do very much good.   But what Mr Harrod had said was true—father was in some way preoccupied.   I think he had had a letter from Frank Forrester about the Children's Charity Houses Scheme, and it had not been a satisfactory one, for when I went into his business-room I found him busily writing to Frank, and I could not get him to pay any attention to me until after post-time.   Then he let me speak.

" Meg, child," he said when I had done,
" I don't feel quite sure that you know a vast
deal yourself about such things; but maybe
you're right in one item, and that is, if I
engage a man to look after my property, I
ought to be willing to abide a bit by his
advice. So we'll have a drop o' tea first,
and then we'll go up and have a look at
these hops of his."

And that is what we did. Mr Harrod
didn't come in to tea, but we met him outside
and walked up the hill together. It was
still that bright June weather of the week
before : we never had so hot and fair a
summer, I believe, as that year. After our
hard long winter, the warmth was new life,
and the long evenings were very exquisite.
The breath of the lilac—just on the wane—
of the bursting syringa, of the heavy daphne,
lay upon the air, and was wafted from behind
garden-walls up the village street.

As we passed the old town-hall and came
out at the end of the road, the white arms
of the mill detached themselves against the
bright sky where the sun, sinking nearer
to the horizon, rayed the west with glory.

Father stood a moment on the crest of the hill looking down into the valley, upon whose confines the broad meads of the South Downs swelled into rising ground again; a stream wound across the plain that was intersected by dykes at intervals; far to the left lay the sea—a dim, blue line across the stems of the trees, breaking into a little bay in the dip of the hill where the valley met the marsh.

"The Elms" stood on the brow of the hill nearer the sea; the hop-gardens that belonged to it lay close at our feet. We went down among the sheep and the sturdy lambs that leapt lightly still after their dams; father walked slowly in front, Mr Harrod and I followed. The hop planta-tions covered the slopes, and swept across the valley to the other side. We passed the house to our left above us, and went down into the valley.

The hops, according to their sort, had grown to various heights—some three feet, some less—and the women and girls from the village had been out during the last month tying them, so that they were now past the second bind.

Father and Mr Harrod walked in a critical way through the lines of plants, examining them carefully. Here and there Trayton Harrod pinched off the flower of a bine that had been left on.

" It's very strange," said he, " that pruning and branching of the hops used not to be done some years ago. I read in an old book that the practice was first introduced since farmers noticed how hailstones, nipping off the bine-tops early in the summer, made the plants grow stronger."

They walked on again, Harrod showing father where the Jones hops grew, and where the Goldings, and arguing that, for purposes of early foreign export, the Jones hops easily took the place of the Early Prolifics, and came to a far finer, taller growth ; while for later introduction into the market, the Goldings were the best grown. Father stated the same objections that Reuben had stated — Trayton Harrod fighting each one vigorously, and coming off victorious, as he somehow always did.

We walked on through the gardens and then up by the house, and back along the brow of the hill.

The sun had sunk below the horizon, and the crimson of the after-glow lay, a lump of fire, in the purple west, and sent rays of redness far into the heavens on every side, washing the clouds with a hundred tints from the brightest rose to the tenderest violet, the faintest green, the softest dove-colour above our heads. Behind the village and its houses a row of dusky-headed pines stood tall or bent their trunks, bowed by the storm-winds, across the road : father stopped there a moment and looked at the glowing sky from between their red stems. The hills lay round the plain, wonderfully blue; the sunset gilded the quiet little stream upon the marsh, till it looked like a streak of molten metal. He had not spoken a word, and now he sighed, half impatiently, as he turned homewards. I remember that Mr Harrod left us at that point. He promised to be in to supper, and father and I walked on alone.

When we got to the dip of the road where the hill begins to go down towards the sea-marsh, we met Mr Hoad coming up in his smart little gig, with his daughter Jessie at his side. I was for passing them with merely a bow, for they showed no signs of stopping, and I desired no conversation with either of them; but father stopped the gig.

" Hoad, can you spare me a few minutes?" asked he. " I should be much obliged to you. Miss Jessie, you'll come in and have a cup of tea," added he courteously.

Miss Jessie said that she should be very pleased to come; but she did not look pleased, and for the matter of that, I fear, neither did I. I could not think why father should want Mr Hoad's company again so soon; but I supposed it must be about that letter of Frank's. He had evidently seemed annoyed about it, although I did not know at that time why it was.

I took Jessie Hoad into the parlour while the two men went into the business-room. Mother was rather flurried when I announced, in my blunt way, that these visitors were going to stay to tea. The presence of a strange woman always *did* trouble mother a bit; and Jessie having been the head of her father's house since her mother died, she considered her in the light of a housewife. I knew that she was longing to have her best china out, and the holland covers off in the front parlour. She was far too hospitable, however, to allow this feeling to be apparent, and she rose at once to welcome her guest.

" I'm very pleased to see you, Miss Hoad," said she ; " I'm sorry Joyce is away."

" Oh, not at all ; pray don't mention it, Mrs Maliphant," declared Jessie, in her hard, high voice, sitting down and settling her dress to advantage. " Of course I'm sorry to miss Joyce, but I'm very glad to see you and Margaret."

My blood boiled to hear her call us like that by our Christian names, and to see the way she sat there with her little smart hat, and her little nose turned up in the air, chatting away to mother in a patronising kind of way, and keeping the talk quite in her own hands with all the town news she had to tell.

" Yes, the Thornes' is a beautiful house," she was saying,—" all in the best style, and quite regardless of expense. I assure you the dessert service was all gold and silver the other night when father and I dined there. Of course it was a grand affair—all the county swells there. But the thing couldn't have been done better in London, I declare."

"Indeed!" answered mother. "I haven't much knowledge of London."

"No, of course not," said Jessie. "But you have seen the Thornes' house, I suppose?"

"No," answered mother. "We don't go there. My husband and Mr Thorne don't hold together."

"Oh, indeed!" exclaimed Jessie,—"that's a pity. He and his daughter are the nicest people in the county. But, as I was saying to Mary Thorne, there's something very quaint in your old house, and I can't help fancying the new style does copy some things from the old houses."

"Oh, I can't believe that," said I, half piqued. "It wouldn't be worth its while."

She looked round at me, a little puzzled, I think; but any rub there might have been between us was put a stop to by the entrance of father and Mr Hoad from the study.

Mr Hoad was, if anything, in better spirits than ever : his eyes were bright, and he rubbed his hands as a man might do when anything had gone to his satisfaction. Father's brow, on the contrary, was heavy. We sat down to tea. Mr Harrod came in a little late. He was about to retire when he saw that we had company; but mother so insisted on his taking his usual seat that it would have been rude to refuse, although I could see that he did not care for the society.

Mother introduced him to Miss Hoad, who just looked up under the brim of her hat, and then went back to her muffin as if none of us were much worth considering. There was altogether an air about her as though she wanted to get over the whole affair as soon as possible. And she did. That bland father of hers had not time for more than half the pleasant things that he usually said to us all before she whipped him off.

"It'll be quite too late to pay our call at 'The Priory' if we don't go at once, papa," said she, rising and looking at a dainty gold watch at her waist. I suppose she did not trust the time of our old eight-day clock that stood between the windows, yet I'll warrant it was the safer of the two.

She turned to mother.

" I'm sorry to have to run away so soon," said she, with an outward show of cordiality, "but you see it's very important to leave cards on people like the Thornes directly after a large party. And if I don't do it to-day, I must drive out again on purpose to-morrow."

" Have you been dining at Thorne's, Hoad ? " asked father.

" Yes," answered the solicitor. " He's a rare good fellow, and he gave us a rare good dinner."

Father did not say a word, and the Hoads took their leave.

" I'll let you have that the first thing in the morning," said Mr Hoad, as he shook hands with father.

Father nodded, but otherwise made no remark. When the visitors were gone he turned to Mr Harrod. " I've made up my mind to rent ' The Elms,' " said he shortly. " We'll drive into town to-morrow and see Searle's executors about it."

" That's right, sir," said Harrod cheerfully.

" I feel sure it will turn out a sound invest-
ment."

" ' The Elms ! ' " exclaimed mother. " Are
you thinking of that, Laban ? "

" Yes," answered he. " Harrod advises
it."

" Well, of course I shouldn't like to set
myself against Mr Harrod," said mother, half
doubtfully. " But I should have thought our
own farm was enough to see after. It seems
a deal of responsibility and laying out of
money."

" There's no farm to speak of at ' The
Elms,' ma'am," answered Harrod. " It's
all hop-gardens. That's why I advised Mr
Maliphant buying it."

" Dear," said mother, nowise reassured.
" Isn't that very risky ? I've always heard
of hops as being riskier than cows, and
I'm sure they're bad enough, though Reuben
will have it they're nothing to sheep at the
lambing."

Harrod had frowned a little at first, but
now he smiled. " There's a risk in everything," he said. " You might break your
leg walking across the room."

"You'll live up at the house, Harrod," put in father. "I've been sorry there's been no better place for you up to the present time."

"Oh, I've done very well," laughed the young man, "but it'll be best I should go over there now. It's only a step for me to get here of mornings."

"Well, I'm glad of *that*, at any rate," said mother. "Father's quite right. It wasn't fitting for you as our bailiff not to have a proper place. And now you'll have it. Meg, you and I must go up and see as everything's comfortable. And we must get a woman in the place to see after him. Old Dorcas's niece might do. She's a widow. She'd want to take her youngest with her, but you wouldn't mind that," added she, turning again to Harrod. Her mind was full of the matter now. So was mine. We were quite at one upon it, and discussed it the whole evening. Nevertheless I found time to wonder now and then how it was that it was only after his talk with Mr Hoad that father had made up his mind to take on "The Elms." It rather riled me. Mr

Hoad could not possibly know as much about farming as did Trayton Harrod.

However, the thing was done, that was the main thing. Mr Harrod had had his wish, and I tried to flatter myself that I was in some way instrumental in procuring it.

CHAPTER XX.

THE time was drawing near when Joyce was to come home, and I had done positively nothing in the matter in which I had promised to fight her battle. It is true that she had begged me not to fight her battle, but I wanted to fight it, and I was vexed with myself that I had so allowed the matter to slide. In the one tussle that I had had with mother, I had been so worsted that I felt, with mortification, my later silence must look like a confession of defeat.

The fact is that I had been thinking of other things. Trayton Harrod and I had had a great many things to think of. He had started a new scheme for the laying on of water.

Our village abounded in wells; they, too, were the remnants of the affluence of the

town in bygone days, but they were all at
the foot of the hill.

Trayton Harrod wanted to bring the
water from the spring at the top of Croft's
hill in pipes through the valley, and up our
own hill again. He wanted to form a co-
operation among the inhabitants for the en-
terprise. If this was impossible, he wanted
father to do it as a private undertaking,
and to repay himself by charging a rental
to those people who would have it brought
to their houses. But he met with opposition
at every turn. The inhabitants of Marshlands were a stubborn lot: they did not
believe in the possibility of the thing; they
did not care for innovations; they had done
very well all these years with carts that
brought the water up the hill and stored
it in wells in their gardens, and why not
now? He had not gained his point yet,
either in one way or in the other, and I had
been very busy fighting it for him; that was
how it had come to pass that I had forgotten
Joyce's business.

Mother and I sat in the low window-seat
of the parlour, straining our eyes over the

mending of the family socks and stockings by the waning light of the June evening. Mother had missed Joyce very much. I had not been all that a daughter should have been to her since I had been in sole charge. I had been preoccupied, and she had missed Joyce much more, I knew very well, than she chose to confess. Knowing this as I did, I thought the moment would be well chosen to speak of what should affect Joyce's happiness. I thought her heart would be soft to her. But on this point I was mistaken. Mother did not alter her opinion because her heart was soft. She could be very tender, but she was most certainly also very obstinate.

I opened the conversation by alluding to the letter which father had had from Captain Forrester.

"That scheme of his for poor children doesn't seem to be able to get started as easily as he hoped," I said. "I'm sorry. It would have been a beautiful thing, and father will break his heart if it falls through."

" He seems to think the young man hasn't gone the right way to work," said mother.

" I could have told him he wasn't the right
sort for the job."

I tried to keep my temper, and it was
with a laugh that I said, "Well, if anything could be done I'm sure he would do
it, if it was only for the sake of pleasing
Joyce."

Mother said nothing. She prided herself
upon her darning, and she was intent upon a
very elaborate piece of lattice-work.

"He would do anything to please Joyce.
I never saw a man so much in love with a
girl," I said.

"Have you had great experience of that
matter?" asked mother in her coolest manner. "Because if you have, I should like to
hear of it : girls of nineteen don't generally
have much experience in such matters."

"I can see that he is in love well enough,"
said I, biting my lip. Then warming suddenly, I added : "I don't see why, mother,
you should set your face so against the young
man? You want Joyce to be happy, don't
you?"

"Yes," said mother quietly, "I want her
to be happy."

"Well, it won't make her happy never to see the man she loves," cried I ; "no, nor yet to have to wait all that time before she can marry him. I've always heard that long engagements were dreadfully bad things for girls."

Mother smiled. " I waited three years for your father," she said, "and I'm a hearty woman of my years."

" Perhaps you were different," suggested I.

" May be," assented mother. "Women weren't so forward-coming in my time, to be sure."

" I don't see that Joyce is forward," cried I.

" No, Joyce is seemly behaved if she is let alone. She'll bide her time, I've no doubt," said mother.

I felt the hidden thrust, and it was the more sharply that I replied—"You're so fond of Joyce, I should have thought you wouldn't care to make her suffer."

Mother gave a little sigh. She took no notice of my rude taunt.

" The Lord knows it's hard to know what's best," said she. " But I'd sooner see her pine a bit now than spend her whole

life in misery ; and there's no misery like that
of a home where the love hasn't lasted out."

The earnestness of this speech made me
ashamed of my vexation, and it was gently
that I said—" But, mother, I don't see why
you should think a man must needs be fickle
because he falls in love at first sight.   I
don't see how people who have known one
another all their lives think of falling in love.
When do they begin ? "

" I don't know as I understand this mighty
thing that you young folk call 'falling in
love,'" said mother.   " I was quite sure
what I was about when I married your
father."

" Well now, mother, I don't see *how* you
can have been quite sure beforehand," argued
I obstinately.   " You have been lucky, that's
all."

" Nay, it's not all luck," said mother.   " It
isn't all plain sailing over fifty or sixty years
of rubbing up and down ; and they'd best
have something stouter than a mere fancy
to stand upon, who want to make a good
job of it."

" I don't see what they are to have stouter

than love to stand upon," said I. "And I
always thought love was a thing that came
whether you would or no, and had nothing
to do with the merits of people."

It was all a great puzzle. Did mother
make too little of love, and did I make too
much ?

" That's not love," said mother,—" that's
a fancy. I misdoubt people who undertake
to show patience and steadiness in one thing,
before they have learnt it in anything else."

" What has Frank Forrester done, I
should like to know ? " asked I, feeling that
she was hard on him.

" Nothing, my dear," answered mother, laconically.

And I sighed. It was very evident there
would be no convincing mother, and that if
there was to be any relaxation in the hard-
ness of the verdict for Joyce, it must come
through father and not through her.

She rose and moved away, for the light
had waned, and we could not see to work.

" If I loved a man I'd take my chance,"
was my parting shot.

" Then, my dear, it's to be hoped you

won't love a man just yet," said mother, as
she went out of the room.

And that was all I got by my endeavour
to further my sister's cause with mother.
I think, however, I soon forgot the annoyance that my failure caused me : it was
driven out of my head by other and more
engrossing interests.

Mother and I had been up at " The Elms "
that very day, getting things in order for Mr
Harrod. We had found a tidy widow woman
to wait on him, and mother had put up fresh
white dimity curtains from her own store to
brighten up his little parlour. When he came
in to supper he was full of quiet delight. I
forget what he said : he was not a man of
many words,—he was always wrapped up in
his business ; but I recollect that, however
few they were, they were words of affectionate
gratitude to mother for a kind of care which
he seemed never to have known before, and
I was grateful to him for them.

So sensitively responsible is one for the
actions of another who is slowly creeping
near to one's heart.

Harrod sat some time with mother on the

lawn discussing the qualities of cows: she
wanted father to give her a new one, and she
wanted Harrod to find her one as good as
Daisy, if such a thing were possible. He
listened with great patience to her reminis-
cences of past favourites, and promised to
do his best; but I could see that there was
something on his mind.

I fell to wondering what it was. I fell to
wondering whether Trayton Harrod ever
thought of anything else but the work he
had to do, the dumb creatures that came his
way in the doing of it, and the fair or lower-
ing face of the world in which he did it. I
soon learned what it was. It was something
that had been discussed many times, but it
had never been discussed as it was discussed
that evening.

Father came out with his pipe a-light: his
rugged old face wore its most dreamy and
contented expression. He had evidently
been thinking of something that had given
him pleasure; but I do not think it had to
do with the farm. But Mr Harrod went to
meet him, and they strolled down the garden
together, and stood for about ten minutes

talking hard by the bed where the golden
gilliflowers and the purple iris bloomed side
by side.

"Well, you know what I have told you,
Mr Maliphant," said Harrod. "You never
can make the farm pay so long as you hold
these theories. Your men work shorter
hours and receive higher wages than anybody else's; and, added to that, you absolutely refuse to have any machinery used.
It'll take you twice as long to get in your
hay and your wheat as it will take the other
farmers. How can you possibly compete
with them ?"

"I don't want to compete with them," said
father — "not in the sense of getting the
better of them. I merely want the farm to
yield me sufficient for a modest living. I
don't need riches."

"Well, and you won't do it in the way
you are going on," said Harrod calmly.
"You won't do so unless you allow me to
stock the farm with the proper machines,
and to get the proper return of labour out
of the men."

"What is the proper return ?" asked

father, his eye lighting up. " That I should get three times the profit the labourer gets ? I'm not sure of it. My capital must be remunerated, of course ; but I am not sure that that is the right proportion." His heavy brows were knit, his hair was more aggressive than ever, his lower lip trembled.

Harrod stared. He had not yet heard father give vent to his theories, and he stared.

"And as for machines," continued father, " I don't choose to have them used, because I consider it unjust that hands should be thrown out of work in order that I may make money the faster. My notions may be quixotic, but they are mine, and the land is mine, and I choose to have it worked according to my wish ! "

" Certainly, sir," answered Harrod stiffly. " Only, as I'm afraid I could not possibly make the farm succeed under these conditions, I would prefer to throw up my situation."

"Very good," said father. " That is as you wish." And he moved on into the house.

Mother looked at Mr Harrod a moment,
as though she were about to beg him to take
no notice and to recall his hasty resignation.   Her eyes had almost a supplicating
look; but apparently she seemed to think
that her appeal would be best made to
father, for she hurried after him through
the open door.

Trayton Harrod and I were left alone on
the terrace.   His mouth was set in a hard
curve, that was all the more apparent for
his clean-shaven chin; his eyes seemed to
have grown quite small.   I was almost afraid
to speak to him.   He stood there a moment,
with his hands in his pockets, looking out
across the marsh where the coming twilight
was already beginning to spread brown
shades, although there was still a reflection
of the distant sunset upon the clouds overhead.   He looked a moment, and then he
turned to go.   But I could not let him go
like that.

My heart had gone down with a sudden
sick feeling when he had said he must leave
Knellestone.   I can remember it now.   I
did not ask myself what it meant.   I sup-

pose I thought, if I thought at all, that it
was anxiety for the welfare of the farm. But
I remember very well how it felt.

"Oh, Mr Harrod, you don't really mean
that!" said I, hurriedly.

"Mean what?" answered he, without re-
laxing a muscle of his face.

"That you will give up your work here."

"Indeed I do," answered he, with a little
hard laugh, showing those white teeth of his.
"A man must do his work his own way, or
not at all."

I did not know what more to say. But
he did not offer to go now : he stood there,
with his hands in his pockets and his back
half turned to me.

"Do you think so?" said I at last, doubtfully.

"Well, if I can't do my work here so that
it should be to your father's advantage, I'm
cheating him, Miss Maliphant—that's evident, isn't it? And I have a particular wish
to be an honest man." There was bitterness
in his voice.

"I see that," said I. "Only, if you go
away the work will be done much less to

father's advantage than if you stay—even
though you can't do it just as you wish."

"That has nothing to do with me," answered Harrod in his hardest voice. "I
should harm my reputation by remaining
here."

A wave of bitterness swept over me too
at that.

"I see," I replied coldly. "You are considering your own interest only. Well, we
have no right to expect any more. You
have only known us a short time."

He did not speak, and I walked forward
to the palisade that hedged the garden and
leant my arms upon it, looking out to the
sea. After a little while he came to my
side.

"Well, you see," said he in a softer voice,
"a man is bound to consider his own interests to that extent at least—so far as doing
his work honestly is concerned. I consider
a man a thief who doesn't do what he has
to do to the best of his lights."

"I quite understand that," answered I.
"I quite understand that it would be more
comfortable for you to go away."

" I should be very sorry to go away," replied he, simply. " I like the place, and I
like the work, and I like the people."

" Then why do you go ? " asked I, bluntly.

" A man must have his convictions," repeated he, doggedly.

I looked up at him now.

" Yes," I said firmly. " Father has his
convictions too. They are not your convictions, but he cares just as much about them.
You ought to make allowances for that."

" I make every allowance for it," answered
he ; " only, I don't see how the two lots can
mix together."

" You said just now that a man must do
his work his own way, or not at all," I went
on, without heeding him. " But I don't see
that."

This time Mr Harrod did more than smile,
he laughed outright. I suppose even in the
short time that we had been friends he had
learnt to know me well enough to see something amusing in my finding fault with any
one for obstinacy. But I was not annoyed
with the laugh ; on the contrary, it restored
my good temper.

"Well, I don't see why you shouldn't go
a little way to meet father," insisted I, boldly.
"Of course he won't give in to you about
everything — it isn't likely he should do.
But you might do a great many things
that he wouldn't mind, which would make
the farm better; and then, when he saw
they made it better, and that the labourers
went on just as well, maybe he would let
you do a few more. I can't discuss it,"
added I, seeing that Harrod was about to
speak, "because I can't understand it. But
I see one thing plain, and that is that folk
think the farm wants doing something with
that father doesn't do—and if so, you're the
man to do it."

I paused. Had I not followed the Squire's
instructions well?   Had I not done my very
best to "smooth over difficulties"?

"I don't think that I am the only man
who could do it, by any means," answered
Harrod.   But he said it doubtfully—pleasantly doubtfully.

It made me bold to retort with greater
determination : "Well, *I* think so, then.   And
if you say you are comfortable here, if you

say you like the place — and the people,"
added I, hurriedly, "why don't you try, at
least, to stay on and help us ? "

He did not reply. We stood there what
must have been a considerable time looking
before us silently. The wane of the day had
fallen into dusk, the brown had settled into
grey, now that the gold of the sunset reflections had faded ; the marsh-land was very
still and sweet, the sheep were not even
white blots upon it, so entirely did the tender
pall harmonise all degrees of hue, so that the
kine seemed no longer as living beings but
as mysterious shapes bred of the very land
itself; even the old castle, so grand and
solid in the daytime, was now like some
phantom thing in the solitude—every curve
and every circle defined more clearly than
in sunlight, yet the whole transparent in
the transparent gloaming of the air.

The most solid thing in all this varied
uniformity, this intangible harmony, was a
clump of trees in the near distance that
told a shade blacker than anything else;
for the turrets of the distant town lay only
as a faint mass of purple upon the land, the

little lights that twinkled in it here and there
alone betraying its nature : long, living lines
of strange clouds, that were neither violet
nor grey nor white, lay along the blue where
sea and sky were one.

"Before you came," said I at last, in a
low voice, "I used to think that I could help
father as well as any *man*. I thought that
I understood very nearly as much about
farming as he did. I thought I could do
much better than a stranger, who would not
understand the land or the people. But now
I think differently. I see how much more
you know than I had dreamed of. You
have made me feel very foolish."

"I'm sorry for that," said he. "It was far
from my intentions — very far from my
thoughts."

He said no more, neither did I. Perhaps,
to tell the truth, I was half sorry for what I
had said, half ashamed of even feeling my
inferiority, more than half ashamed of having
confessed it to any one. Ashamed, sorry—
and yet——?

Mother called us to go indoors.

"If your father asks me to remain, I will

remain and do my best," said Trayton Harrod as we walked slowly up the lawn.

And the glow that was upon my heart
deepened.   It was a concession, and where-
fore was it made?

CHAPTER XXI.

For two days not a word was spoken on the sore subject between father and Mr Harrod, and on the evening of the second day the Squire returned from town.

Father and I had gone down on the morning after the quarrel to see the sheep-shearing at the lower farm. By a corruption of the name of a former owner the country folk had come to call it " Pharisee Farm," and Pharisee Farm it always was. It lay on the lower strip of marsh towards the castle, with the southern sun full upon it. As we came down the hill I heard steps behind us, and without turning I knew that Trayton Harrod was following us. Father gave him good day quite civilly, and I held out my hand. I do not know why I had got into the habit of giving my hand to Trayton Harrod; it was not a usual habit with me.

"It has turned a bit cooler, Mr Maliphant, hasn't it?" said Harrod.

"Yes," answered father; "but we must be glad we have had the rain before we had to get the hay in."

"That we must," replied Harrod. "The hay looks beautiful."

We were passing along through the meadows ready for the scythes; they stretched on every side of us. Meadows for hay, pastures for sheep, there was scarcely anything else, save here and there a blue turnip-field or a tract of sparsely-sown brown land where the wheat made as yet no show. The one little homestead to which we were bound made a very poor effect in the vast plain: there was nothing but land and sea and sky. A great deal of land, flat monotonous land—more monotonous now in its richness, and the brilliant greenness of its early summer-time, than it would be later when the corn was ripe and the flowering grasses turning to brown: an uneventful land, relying for its impressiveness on its broad simplicity that seemed to have no reason for ending or change; above the great stretch of

earth a great vault of blue sky flecked with
white vapours and lined with long opal
clouds out towards the horizon; between
the land and the sky, a strip of blue
sea binding both together,—sea, blue as a
sapphire against the green of the spring
pastures. Far down here upon the level we
could not see the belt of yellow shingle that
from the cliff above one could tell divided
marsh and ocean : right across the wide space
it was one stretch of lightly varied tints, away
to the shipping and the scattered buildings
at the mouth of the river.

We walked on, three abreast. Our talk
was of nothing in particular; only of the
budding summer flowers — yellow iris and
meadow - sweet along the dykes, crowsfoot
making golden patches on the meadows,
scarlet poppies beginning to appear among
the growing wheat. But I don't know how
it was that, in spite of father's presence, there
was a kind of feeling in my heart as though
Trayton Harrod and I were quite on a different plane to what we had been two days ago :
I don't know why it was, but I was very
happy.

The sheep were gathered in the fold when we reached the farm, and Tom Beale the shepherd was clipping them with swift and adroit hands. Reuben and his old dog Luck were there also; they were both of them very fond of having a finger in the pie of their former calling, but I think there was no love lost between them all. Luck could be good friends enough with Taff, but he never could abide that smart young collie who followed Tom Beale's lead; and as for Reuben, he was busy already passing comments in a low voice to father on the way in which Beale was doing his work.

Father humoured the old man to the top of his bent—he was very fond of Reuben,—but Beale went his way all the same, and sent one poor patient ewe after another out of its heavy fleece, to leap, amazed and frightened, among the flock, unable to trace its companions in their altered condition. One could scarcely help laughing, they looked so naked and bewildered reft of their warm covering, and just about two-thirds their usual size.

"Ay, the lambs won't have much more

good o' their dams now," chuckled Reuben. "They're forced to wean themselves, most on them, after this, for there are few enough that knows one another again."

"They do look different, to be sure," laughed I.

"You might get your 'tiver' now, Reuben Ruck," said Beale, "if you have a mind to give a hand with this job. They're most on 'em tarred."

The "tiver" was the red chalk with which the sheep were to be marked down their backs, or with a ring or a half-ring round their necks, according to the kind and the age. A shepherd had been tarring them on their hindquarters with father's initials, each one as it leapt from out of its fleece.

The work went on briskly for a while, and we were all silent watching Reuben mark the two- and three- and four-year olds apart.

"It's a pity there aren't more Southdowns among the flock," put in Harrod at last.

I turned round and looked at him warningly. It was a mistake, I thought, that, under the strained relations of the moment, he should choose to open up another vexed question.

"Southdowns!" echoed Reuben, who was listening. "You'd drop a deal o' master's money if you began getting Southdowns into his flocks."

I bit my lip, furious with the old servant for his officiousness; but to my surprise father himself reprimanded him sharply for it, and, turning to his bailiff, led him aside a few steps and discussed the question with him at length. My heart glowed with pleasure as I overheard him commission Harrod to go to the fair at Ashford next week and see if he could effect some satisfactory purchase. I was quite pleased to note Reuben's surly looks. How sadly was I changing to my old friends! And yet so much more pleased was I to see the honest flush of satisfaction on Harrod's face as father left him, that I felt no further grudge against the old man, and nodded to him gaily as I followed father across the marsh.

When we reached the bottom of the hill we met the Squire. He was coming down the road full tilt with the collie who was his constant companion, and before we came

within earshot I could see that his face was
troubled.   I knew him well enough now to
tell when he was troubled.

"Why, Maliphant, what's this I hear?"
said he, as he came up to us.

Father leaned forward on his stick, looking
at the Squire with a half-amused, half-defiant
expression in his eyes.

"Well, Squire Broderick, what is it?"
asked he.

"I hear in the village that you have leased
'The Elms,'" answered the other, almost
severely.

I happened to be looking at father, and I
could see that his face changed.

"Yes," he said quietly, "I have. What
then?"

The Squire laughed constrainedly.

"Well," he began, and then he stopped,
and then he began again. "'Tis a large
speculation. What made you think of it?"

"Mr Harrod advised father to take on
'The Elms,'" I put in quickly. I was
vexed with the Squire for saying anything
that was a disadvantage to Trayton Harrod
in the present state of affairs.

"Harrod!" cried the Squire. He began beating his boot with his stick in that way he had when he was annoyed. "I thought it was Hoad," he said at last beneath his breath.

Father's eyes were black beads. "Pray don't trouble yourself to think who it was who advised me, Squire," said he. "If it's a bad speculation nobody is to blame but myself. I am entirely my own master. I was told 'The Elms' was to be had, and I chose to take it. My hop-gardens were not as extensive as I wished."

He had raised his voice involuntarily in speaking. A man passing in the road turned round and looked at him.

"Hush, father," whispered I.

It was one of his own labourers, one of father's special friends.

"Wait a bit, Joe Jenkins, I'm coming up the road. I want a word with you," said father.

He held out his hand to the Squire, but without looking at him, and then went on up the hill. I stayed a moment behind. The Squire looked regularly distressed.

"Your father is so peppery," he said,—
"so very peppery."

"Well, I don't understand what you mean,"
said I, but not in allusion to his last remark.
"Why isn't the thing a good speculation?"

"Oh, my dear young lady, it's very difficult
to tell what things are going to turn out to
be good speculations and what not," answered
he. "At all events, I'm afraid you and I
would not be able to tell."

It was very polite of him, no doubt, to put
it so, but I did not like it: it seemed making fun of me, for of course no one had
said that I should be able to tell.

"I understood that you thought a great
deal of Mr Harrod's judgment," said I,
coldly.

"So I do, so I do," repeated the Squire
eagerly. "I believe it to be most sound."

"Well, anyhow father won't have it much
longer, sound or unsound, unless things take
a different turn," continued I, with a grim
sense of satisfaction in hurting the Squire
for having hurt Harrod's case with father.

"Why, what's up?" asked he.

"They have had a quarrel," explained I,

carelessly. " Mr Harrod wanted father to
reduce the men's wages, and to make them
work as long hours as they do for the other
farmers hereabouts, and of course father
wasn't going to do that, because he thinks
it unjust."

" I knew it would come—bound to come,"
muttered the Squire beneath his breath.

" And then he wanted him to buy mowing-
machines for the haymaking," continued I,
"and you know what father thinks of
machines. So he refused, and then Mr
Harrod said that if he couldn't manage the
farm his own way he must leave."

" Dear ! dear ! " sighed good Mr Broderick.
And dear me, how little I realised at the time
all that it meant, his taking our affairs to
heart as he did. " This must be set straight."

" I tried my best," concluded I. " It's no
good talking to father ; but Mr Harrod promised me that he would take back his word
about leaving if father asked him to."

The Squire looked at me sharply. " Harrod promised you that ? " he asked.

" Yes," repeated I, looking at him simply,
"he promised me that."

The Squire said no more, but his brow was knit as he turned away from me.

"I'll go and see Harrod," said he. "Can you tell me at all where I shall find him?"

"He's down at Pharisee farm at the sheep-shearing," said I. "He and Reuben are having a quarrel over Southdowns. He wants to have Southdowns in the flock. But if he goes away there'll be no Southdowns needed."

Mr Broderick made no answer to this,— he strode on down the road. But when he had gone a few steps he turned.

"By-the-by, will you tell your father," he said, "that my nephew came down with me last night. I believe he wants to see him on some affair or other. No doubt he'll call round in the afternoon."

He went on quickly, and I stood there wondering. Frank Forrester back again at the Manor! Did he suppose that Joyce had returned? Did he hope to see her? Poor fellow! He little knew mother.

"Father," said I, as I joined him on the hill, "do you know that Captain Forrester has come down again?"

He stopped—he was a little out of breath ;
I even fancied that his cheek was flushed.

" You don't say so," said he. " He gave me
no idea of it in his letter—no idea at all."

A light had kindled in his eye.

" When does your sister come home ? " he
asked.

" She was to have come next week," answered I. " But I suppose mother will put
it off now."

" Yes, Meg," said he, with a twinkle in
his eye, " I suppose she'll put it off. And
yet the lad is a good lad ; but mother knows
best, mother knows best."

We turned up the road, and as we came
to the corner of the village street we saw
two figures coming along towards us. One
of them was Mary Thorne, and the other
was Captain Forrester. I had not known
the Thornes were back at the Priory : they
had left it for the London season.

The two were laughing and talking gaily.
She came forward cordially as soon as she saw
me, and held out her hand. Her round, rosy
face shone with merriment, and her brown
hair caught the sunlight. She spoke to me

first, while Frank was shaking father warmly
by the hand.

"How are you, Mr Maliphant?" cried
he. "It's delightful to see you again. You
see I could not keep away. I had to come
down and get a fresh impetus, fresh instructions."

Mary Thorne laughed. "Oh, he talks of
nothing else," said she. "He's quite crazed
over this wonderful scheme, I can assure you,
Mr Maliphant."

Father's brow clouded, and to be sure
I could not bear to hear her talk like that,
though why, I could not exactly have told.

"And so we made it an excuse to snatch
a couple of days from balls and things, and
come down here for a breath of fresh air,"
she continued.

I wondered why she said "we." But
Frank explained that.

"Mr Thorne is quite interested in the
affair, I can assure you, Mr Maliphant," said
he. "He's going to put a splendid figure to
head our subscription list."

Father did not say a word. His shaggy
eyebrows were down over his eyes.

"Oh, well, father never is stingy with his money—I must say that for him," said Mary. "He'll give anything to anything." Then turning to me, she added, "We're going to squeeze in a garden-party next week, before we run up to town again. They say one must give entertainments this electioneering time. At least that Mr Hoad says so, and he seems to have done a great deal of this kind of thing, from what he says. We did two dinners before we went up to London, but a garden-party is jolly — it includes so many. You'll come, won't you—all of you? You're just about the only people I care to ask, you know."

She ran on in her frank, funny way—always quite transparent—not noticing father's scowl and Frank Forrester pulling his moustache, and trying to catch her eye. If she had, she would have turned the matter off: she was no fool, but what she had said was what she thought.

Father answered before I could speak. "My eldest daughter is away, Miss Thorne," he said, "and I'm sorry to say Margaret must refuse your kind invitation. My girls are farmer's children, and are not used to mixing with folk in other stations of life."

I felt the colour fly to my face, for it was a discourteous speech, and not even per-fectly honest, for Mary Thorne had met us at the Squire's house although we *were* only farmer's daughters. It mortified me to have father do himself injustice before Frank Forrester.

But Mary took it charmingly. For a moment she looked astonished; then she said, with a merry laugh, "Ah, I see what it is, Mr Maliphant—you're a Tory. I beg your pardon; I forgot you were the Squire's friend. I'm dreadfully stupid about politics. I'm quite ashamed of myself."

Father seemed about to reply, but was stopped by a merry laugh from Frank, whom Mary, however, silenced by a pretty little astonished stare.

"Oh, pray don't apologise," said she to father. "Only don't you try to tell me another time that your daughters are not used to good society. I know better," added she, smiling at me. "I know who was voted the best dancer at the Squire's

ball. And as for your eldest daughter—
well, we know how many heads *she* has
turned with her beauty."

She glanced up teasingly at Captain Forrester as she spoke. She was a little woman,
and had to glance up a long way; but although he laughed, his face was troubled,
and I could see he was trying to catch my
eye.

" Well, good-bye," said Mary to me. " I'm
sorry you mayn't come."

I took the hand which she offered, but
when she held it out afterwards to father,
he only bowed with laborious politeness. I
think I blushed with annoyance as we turned
away, but he made no allusion to the meeting; only his brightened humour of five minutes ago had evaporated, and his features
were working painfully.

" I shall go and fetch little David Jarrett,
Meg," said he. " The sun is warm now, and
it'll do him good to lie a bit in the garden.
Go home and tell mother."

I went, and a quarter of an hour later he
carried the boy in—a poor little delicate fellow, whose father had knocked him down in

a drunken fit, and who had been a cripple
ever since. We had heard of the misfortune
too late to be of much use, for continued
want of proper nourishment on a sickly
frame had caused the accident to set up
a disease from which the poor child was
scarcely likely to recover; but all that could
be done father had had done, and he was
his special favourite among many friends in
the younger portion of the community. We
spread a mattress on the garden bench and
laid him there, and mother sent me out with
port wine and strengthening broth for him,
and father spent all the afternoon beside the
little fellow, reading and talking to him.

Beyond alluding to Captain Forrester's
arrival when mother spoke of it, he made
no mention of his young friend or of what
had hurt him in the passing meeting with
him. But when Frank came as promised in
the evening, the storm broke.

He came in just as if he had not been
away from us these two months; just as
kindly, just as interested in all we had been
doing, just as easy and charming. But when,
I fancied a trifle diffidently, he opened up the

subject of the charity scheme, father suffered no misunderstanding to abide.

"I know Thorne is an old friend of your family's, my lad," he said, "and I understand that you can't throw off an acquaintance of your youth; but as to this affair, I want to make it quite clear that I'll have no influence of his to start the school with. If I could help it I'd have none of his money. I can't help that, and the 'big figure' must stand, but I'll have none of him or the likes of him on any committee that may be formed, not while I'm in it."

Father always became vernacular when he was excited

"Very well, sir," smiled Frank. "It's your affair, and I must be led by you. I think you're mistaken. You miss the valuable help of a large and influential class; and why you should forbid manufacturers to remedy an evil which they may have been partly instrumental in increasing, I don't know. But you have your reasons, and I am in your hands."

"Yes, I have my reasons," repeated father laconically.

And then the conversation became general,
and Frank, with his usual amiable courtesy,
drew Trayton Harrod into it, as far as the
somewhat morose mood of the latter would
allow. He seemed to have taken no fancy
to the new-comer, and responded but surlily
to his interested questions upon the country
and country matters.

Frank Forrester was always interested in
everything,—always seemed to be most so in
the subject which he thought interested the
particular person to whom he was speaking.
But Harrod would betray no enthusiasm on
his own pursuits to an outsider. He was
very surly that night. I think he was not
well. Mother taxed him with it. As I have
said, she took a motherly interest in him
always. He allowed that he had a bad
headache, and rose to leave. I recollect
that she went up-stairs to fetch him some
little medicament. Father, too, followed him
out into the hall. They stood there some
five minutes talking, during which time I am
afraid that I tried more to listen to what they
were saying than to what Frank Forrester
took the opportunity to say to me.

I brought my mind to it, however, and told him what I could about Joyce. There was so little to tell; there was always so little to tell about Joyce—nothing very satisfactory to a lover in this instance.

And I was forced to allow what he half gaily asserted — that mother was none the more cordial to him than she had been in the past. He did not seem to be cast down about it, he only asserted it. He did not seem to be in any way cast down. He looked at me with those wide-open brown eyes just as confidently and gaily as ever, and bent towards me with his tall, slim, lissome figure, and took my two hands in his and told me to tell Joyce that he had come hoping to see her for a moment, even though it had been but in mother's presence.

"She forbade me to see her against your mother's wishes," said he, "but openly there would have been no harm."

I felt quite sure that he loved her just as much as ever, and I willingly promised to give his messages to her.

But I hurried over the little interview. I wanted to get out into the hall before Harrod left, and I shook hands with Frank hastily as I heard mother coming down-stairs with the physic.

I was too late nevertheless. Frank had kept me for a last word, and the front door closed as I came out of the room. I went up to bed in a bad temper.

CHAPTER XXII.

TRAYTON HARROD did not leave Knellestone.
I think we had to thank the Squire for that.
Father and he being so proud and obstinate,
they would never have come to an under-
standing alone, nor would either certainly
have accepted me for a mediator.

I don't know whether Mr Broderick persuaded father to ask his bailiff to remain, or
how the matter was arranged. I only know
that a few days after the Squire's return, I
met Harrod down at the haymaking on the
eastern marsh, and that he told me he was not
going to leave us. I remember very well
how he told it me, with a smile ; not that quick
flash which I have sometimes noticed before
as being characteristic of him when moved
to sudden mirth, but a kind of half smile
that had something triumphant in it.

"Yes," he said, looking round on the meadows that were ready for the scythe, "we shall have a mowing-machine on them before the week's out."

That was all; but the words told me he was going to remain. I know I looked up with an answering smile of satisfaction, but it faded as I saw Jack Barnstaple's gloomy eye fixed on me. The very silence of a faithful servant reproved me for my disloyalty. For in my first content I had forgotten that satisfaction to such a speech *was* disloyalty to father, to the horror of machines that had always been my creed till now.

"I'm sorry——" I began, but then I stopped, confused. I was too honest to tell a lie. How could I say that I was sorry he had triumphed? He turned and said some word to the labourer, and I had time to lose my sudden blushes. Had he noticed them? I think I scarcely cared. I was strangely happy.

All that day I was happy. In the eventide we followed the last waggon up the hill. Tired horses, teased to madness by the oxfly in the heat, tired men shouldering their forks, tired women in curious sun-bonnets, and girls not too tired yet to laugh with the lads, went before, and we two followed afterwards, not at all tired of anything—at least, I speak for myself.

A long line of flame marked the horizon behind the hill; and, upon the red sky, the houses of the village, the three roofs and the square tower of the old church, the ivied greyness of the ancient gateway, and the solitary pines that marked the ridge here and there, all lay dark upon the brightness, their shapes defined and single. Close behind us the sea was cool and fragrant. Upon the hem of the wide soft sands that shone in sunset reflections, a regal old heron had fetched his evening meal from out of the little pools that the sea had left, and, unfolding his huge pinions, sailed away in a queer oblique and apparently leisurely flight to the tall trees that were his inland home. We left the haymakers to take the road, and followed the heron across the marsh.

A wheat-ear's nest that I found in a furrow, and carried home with its five little dainty blue eggs, gave rise to a discussion about the rarity of these pretty little struc- tures compared with the numbers of the tiny builders who are so plentiful in harvesting that the shepherds make quite a perquisite from the sale of them; an old hare that the bailiff started from its form on the unbeaten track made him wonder at the unusual size of these marsh inhabitants; and as we came along the dyke where the purple reeds were already growing tall, I remember his no- ticing how changing was their colour on the surface as they swayed in great waves be- neath the breeze,—how blue one way, how silver-grey the other : I recollect every word that we spoke.

It was commonplace talk enough, but it was the talk that had first begun to bind us together, and now there was beginning to be something in it that made every word very much the reverse of commonplace to me. What was it?

I did not ask myself, but I knew very well that since that night when Trayton Harrod had promised to try and remain on at Knellestone, because I had asked him to

do so, that something had grown very fast—
so fast, that I was conscious of a happy state
of guilt, and wondered whether old Deborah
knew anything about it as she watched me
bid the bailiff good-bye at the gate while
she was picking marjoram on the cliff-garden
above our heads.

I know that at first I was angry because
of her keen, little, dark eyes, and her short
little laugh, and I loftily refused to discuss
either with her or with Reuben the advan-
tages of Mr Harrod's remaining on the farm,
or the indignity of having machinery at
Knellestone and Southdowns on the marsh.

There was no delay about either of these
matters. Mr Harrod was a prompt man. I
recollect the very day he bought the sheep,—
yes, I recollect it very well. It was a very
hot day, one of the first days of July. He
had had the mare—my restive mare—put
into the gig, and had started off very early
in the morning to Ashford market. It was
a long way to Ashford market, but you could
just do it and get back in the day if you
started very early, and if you had a horse
like my mare to go. There was a haze over

the sea and even over the marsh : down in
the hayfield, where I had been all the morning, the heat was almost unbearable.   When
five o'clock came, I went in to mother in the
parlour.

"It's such a nice evening for a ride,
mother," said I.   "I think I'll just take
that pot of jelly over to Broadlands to old
Mrs Winter.   She'd be pleased to see
me."

Mother looked up surprised.   "I thought
you didn't care for riding that old horse,"
said she.

"Well, I *can't* have the mare, so it's no use
thinking of it," I answered.

"You can't have her to-day, because the
bailiff has got her, but you can have her to-
morrow," said mother.   "And it's full late
to start off so far."

I walked to the window and looked out.
"I think I'll go to-day," said I.   "It may
blow up for rain to-morrow.   As likely as
not we shall have a storm.   "It's light now
till after nine."

"Very well," said mother.   "You can
please yourself.   You'd better take some of

that stuff for the old body's rheumatism as well."

So I put on my habit and set out.   It was quite true that the old black horse did not go so well as the mare, but, for some reason best known to myself, I had a particular desire to ride to Broadlands that particular afternoon.

I let the poor beast go at his own pace, however, for the heat was still very great : the plain was opal-tinted with it, and the long, soft, purple clouds above the sea hori-zon had a thundery look.   I jogged along dreamily until I was close beneath the old market-town upon the hill.   Somehow the memory of that winter drive with Joyce when we had first met Captain Forrester came back to me vividly.   I don't know how it was, but I began to think of how he had looked at her,—of how he had bent towards her hand just a moment longer than was necessary in parting from her.   I won-dered if those were always the signs of love. I wondered if a man might possibly be in love and yet give none of those signs.

I rode on slowly watching the rising breeze

sweep across the meadows, swaying the long
grass in a rhythmic motion like the waves
of a gentle sea.   I had passed the town by
this time, and had come down the little street
paved with cobble-stones, and through the
grim old gate on to the marsh again.   The
river ran turbidly by, between its mud banks
and across its flat pastures to the sea a mile
beyond.   Above the river the houses of the
town stood, in steps, up the hill, flanked by
the dark-grey stone of the old prison-house,
and crowned by the church with its quaint
flying buttresses ; the wall of the battlements
hemmed the town ; beneath it lay the marsh
and then the sea.

This was all behind me : around and in
front was the faint, grey, flat land, scarcely
green under the creeping haze of heat, with
the breeze undulating over the long grass,
and the lighthouse, the brightest spot on the
scene, as it shone white through the mist on
the distant point of beach.

I took the shortest way, avoiding the
regular road, and was soon lost upon the
grassy sea.   The soft, bright monotony of
the landscape was scarcely broken by a

single incident, save for the martello towers that stood at regular intervals along the coast, or the sheep and cows that were strewn over the pasture - land lazily cropping and chewing the cud. There was not a house within sight, and even the low line of the downs had dipped here into the flatness of the marsh.

I tried to whip the horse into a canter, but the poor beast felt the heat as I did, and I soon let him fall again into his own jog-trot. It was not at all my usual method of riding, but that day I did not mind it so much. I had my thoughts to keep me busy. They were pleasant thoughts—if so vague a dream was a thought at all—and kept me good company. The dream was a dream of love, but I am not sure whether that time Joyce was the heroine. I think, if I had been asked, that I should have said that there was no heroine to my dream—that it was far too vague, too entirely a dream, to have one.

I rode on for another hour across the hot plain before I came to the village of Broadlands. It lay there sleepily upon the bosom

of the marsh, with scarce a tree to shelter it
from the fierce midsummer sun or the wild
sea winds ; and until my horse's hoofs were
clattering up the little street, I scarcely saw
man, woman, or child to tell me that the
place was alive.   But around the "Woolsacks" some half-dozen men lounged, smoking, and a fat farmer in a cart had stopped in
the middle of the road to exchange a few
observations on agricultural news.   It was
the inn at which Trayton Harrod must have
put up in the middle of the day for dinner.

This farmer had evidently returned from
market.   I wondered how long it would be
before Trayton Harrod would also come
along the same road and stop at the
"Woolsacks" for a drink ?   I don't think
I deceived myself as to there being a little
hope within me that I might meet him some-
where on the road.   But I reckoned that he
could not possibly be as far on his homeward
route yet awhile, for he probably had had
much farther to come than the farmer in
the-cart, and had not reached the market
so early.

I trotted on up the street to Mrs Win-

ter's cottage, which stood at the extreme end
of the village, looking out along the Ashford
road. I am afraid that all the time I was
in the cottage—although I gave all mother's
messages, and inquired with due attention
after every one of the old lady's distinct
pains—my eyes were ever wandering along
that dusty road and listening for horse's
hoofs in the distance.

But Mrs Winter noticed no remissness on
my part—she was too pleased to see me, too
glad to have news of mother, who had been
her friend and benefactress these many years
past. I took her a pair of stockings that I
had knit for her in the long winter evenings,
and I can remember now the matter-of-fact
way in which she received the gift, and how,
when I said that I hoped they would fit, she
answered with happy trustfulness—" Oh yes,
miss ; the Lord, He knows my size."

We drank tea out of the white-and-gold
cups that had been best ever since I could
remember ; and then she kissed me and bade
me be going, lest the darkness should over-
take me.

I laughed, and declared that the long twi-

light would more than last me home, for I
did not want to be going until I was sure
that Mr Harrod was on my road : the vague
hope that I had had of meeting him had
grown into a settled determination to wait
for him if I could. But the old lady would
not be pacified by any assurances that I
was not afraid of darkness; and to be sure,
there was a strange shade in the air as I got
outside and mounted the black horse again.

When I got beyond the village again I
saw what it was—there was a sea-fog creeping up the plain. Such fogs were common
enough in the hot weather, and gave me no
concern at all; but I saw, with some dismay,
that the sun must have set some time, for
the twilight was falling in the clear space that
still existed above the mist.

I looked back upon the road. Surely he
could not have passed. I could not bear to
give up the hope of this ride home with him,
and yet I scarcely dared loiter lest mother
should grow anxious. I put the beast to
a gentle trot and rode forward slowly. I
knew of no other way that Harrod could
have taken, and I felt sure that he had

not passed that cottage without my knowledge.

But the mist thickened. I could not see
before me or behind; it was not until I was
close upon it that I could tell where the path
branched off that led across the meadows to
the town. It did not strike me at the time
that I was foolish to take it: I only wondered whether Harrod would be sure to
come that way. I only thought of whether
I should recognise the sound of the mare's
trot, for that was the only means by which
I could be sure of his approach before he
was close upon me.

I rode on slowly, listening always. I rode
on for what seemed to me to be a very long
time. The mist was chill after the hot day,
and I had no covering but my old, thin, blue
serge habit, which had seen many a long
day's wear.

The fog gathered in thickness, and dark-
ened with the darkness of the coming night.
I began to think that, after all, I had made
a mistake in taking the short cut. Perhaps
Mr Harrod had kept to the high-road, as
safer on such a night; perhaps thus I should

miss him. I was not at all afraid of the
fog, but I was very much afraid of missing
the companion for whose sake I had come
this long ride on a hot day. And with the
fear in my mind that I might miss him, I
did a very foolish thing—I turned back upon
my steps. I put the horse to a canter, and
turned back to regain the high-road. I rode
as fast as I could now, urging the beast forward; but though I rode for a much longer
distance than I had ridden already since I
left Mrs Winter's cottage, I saw no trace of
the road.

I stood still at last, and tried to determine
where I was. My heart was beating a little.
Presently—through the stillness, for the air
was absolutely lifeless—I heard the sound of
voices. I listened eagerly. But, alas! there
was no sound of horse's hoofs: the wayfarers,
whoever they were, were on their feet. Mr
Harrod could scarcely be one of them. I
stopped, waiting for them to come up. They
were tramps. Their figures looked waver-
ing and uncertain as they came towards
me through the mist. They walked with a
heavy lounging gait, smoking their clay pipes.

"Can you tell me if I'm in the right way
for the high-road?" said I, as they came
within ear-shot.

They stopped, and one of them burst into
a laugh and said something afterwards in an
undertone to his companion.

"You're a long way from wherever it is
you're bound for," said he; and as he spoke
he came up to me and took hold of the
horse's bridle.

Something in his face displeased me. I
gave him a sharp cut across it with my whip.
He yelled with rage, but he let go the bridle;
and another cut across the horse's neck sent
him forward with his hind hoofs in the air.
I had never known him answer like that to
the whip before. I think he can have liked
the look of the men no better than I did.

Before I knew that there was a dyke
before me, I found myself safely landed on
the other side of it; and it was only then
that I pulled the poor old beast up and
looked round. Of course I could see nothing : the mist would have been too thick,
even had the growing darkness not been
sufficient to obscure any object not close at

hand.   But I could hear no voices, and I felt
that I was safe.

How a girl, with nothing but a little whip
in her hand, had prevailed against two strong
men—even though she was on a horse and
they on foot—I did not pause to consider.
I was safe: but the little adventure had
frightened me, and I thought I would try to
get home as fast as I could.

But how?   I was absolutely uncertain
where I was.   I had crossed a dyke, which I
should not have done; but one dyke was
much like another, and that was no guide.
I could see nothing, and I could hear nothing.

Nothing?   Yes; as I listened I did hear
something.   It was the sound of distant
waves lapping gently upon the beach.   I
must indeed have strayed far from the high-
road if I had come near enough to the sea to
hear the sound of its waves.   I stopped and
waited again.   I thought I would wait until
those men had got well ahead.   Then, after
a while, I put the horse across the dyke again,
and went forward slowly, straining every
nerve to determine whether the sound of the
sea was growing louder or less in my ears.

I felt sure after a while that it was growing less, and yet I could not be absolutely certain, for there was a strange feeling in my head; and I was soon obliged to acknowledge to myself that I was getting very sleepy. The mist, I knew, was apt to make people sleepy if they were out long in it; but I had often been out in a sea-fog before, and I had never felt so sleepy. I wondered what o'clock it was. I struggled on a little longer, but I felt that unless I were to walk I should fall off the horse, so I got down and led him on by the bridle. For another reason it was better to walk—I was chilled to the bone.

I turned the end of my habit up over my shoulders, and although it was wringing wet, it served as a kind of poultice; but I cannot say that I was either cheerful or comfortable. The night was perfectly still, the mist perfectly dense. Once a hare, startled I suppose by the sound of the horse's hoofs, ran across in front of me, and retreated into his form; but I think that that was the only time I saw a living thing.

I got so used to the silence and loneliness, that when at last another sound began to

mingle with the monotonous tread of the
weary beast, I scarcely noticed it. Perhaps
it was because it was only an increase of the
same sound : it was the tread of another
weary beast.   But whether that was the
reason, or whether it was that I was gradu-
ally growing more and more sleepy, certain
it is that the sound grew to a point, and then
began slowly to fade away again before I
was quite conscious of its existence.   Then
suddenly I realised what it might be, and
with all the strength of my being I shouted
through the mist.

Once—twice I shouted, and then I stood
still and listened.   The sound of the hoofs
and the wheels—yes, the wheels—still went
on faintly.   My heart grew sick, and again
I shouted into the night; this time it was
almost a cry.   The wheels stopped.   I shouted again, and there came back a faint holloa
that told me how much fainter still must have
been my own voice through the fog.

I leapt on to the horse, and urged him
forward as near as I could tell in the
direction of the voice.   And all the time I
continued shouting.

Thank heaven! I heard the answering cry clearer and clearer each time. At last —at last I saw a horse and gig just discernible through the steaming darkness.

"Who is there?" cried a voice; and— how can I describe my happiness?—it was the voice of Trayton Harrod.

I don't think I answered. I think there was something in my throat which prevented me from answering, but he must have recognised me at once, for he gave vent to an exclamation which I had never heard him use before — he said, "Great heavens!" Then he got down out of the gig, and came towards me quickly.

"Miss Margaret!" he exclaimed. "How did you ever get here?"

I had recovered my usual voice by this time, and I replied, quietly enough, to the effect that I had been on an errand to Broadlands, and had lost myself coming home in the fog.

"Lost yourself! I should think you had lost yourself," ejaculated he, half angrily. "I was uncertain of my own road before you called, but I know well enough that you are entirely out of the beaten track here."

"Oh! then I'm afraid I shall have made you miss your way too," said I apologetically.

I don't know what had come to me, but I was so glad to see him that I could not bear he should be angry with me.

"That doesn't signify in the least," said he. "It's you of whom I am thinking. I am afraid you must be cold and tired, and I fear we shall be a long while getting home yet." He was close to me now. "You had better get into the gig," said he. "I'll tie the horse to it."

He held out his hands to help me down, and I put mine in his.

"Why, you are chilled to the bone," murmured he. "You'll take your death of cold."

He lifted me from the horse, for indeed I was numb with the penetrating damp, and led me to the gig. Then he took the horse-cloth which lay across the seat and wrapped it round me as tightly as he could.

"Haven't you a pin?" he asked.

I tried to laugh, but I could not; something stuck in my throat.

" I thought women always had pins," he added.

Then I did laugh a little ; but I must have been very much tired and overwrought, for the laugh turned into a sort of sob. I could only hope he did not notice it. He made no remark, at all events; he only wrapped the rug as closely as he could around me, and took hold of my hands again as though to feel if they were any warmer. He held them in his own a long time—he held them very fast. The blood seemed to ebb away from my heart as I stood there with my hands in his. My face was turned away, but I felt that his keen dark eyes were fixed upon mine—concerned-ly, tenderly. A strange new happiness filled my whole being. I did not know what it meant, but I knew that I wanted to keep on standing there like that, in spite of the cold and the dampness and the dark. I knew that what I felt was sweeter than any joy that had come to me before in my life.

But Trayton Harrod took away his hands. He passed his arm round my waist, and holding me by my elbows so as not to displace the plaid which he had wrapt so

carefully around me, he helped me up into
the gig. I let him do just what he liked.
I, who had been so defiant and proud before,
and who thought that I scorned such a thing
as a beau—I was letting this man behave to
me just as Captain Forrester might have behaved to Joyce. I was as wax in his hands.
I did not think of that at the time. I do
not know that I ever thought of it. It only
strikes me now as I write it down.

I sat there without saying a word while
Harrod fetched the horse and tied him to
the back of the gig. I was not conscious of
anything, save that I was perfectly contented, and waiting for him to come up and
sit beside me. All my fatigue had disap-
peared, all my desire to be home, all my
remembrance of mother's anxiety.

But why should I dwell further upon all
this? If any one ever reads what I have
written, they will understand what I felt far
better than I can describe it. Every one
knows that love is self-absorbed, and, save
towards the one being for whom it would
sacrifice all the world, utterly selfish. And
what I was slowly beginning to feel was love.

We moved away into the misty night.
Mr Harrod did not speak for some time.
He was busy enough trying to find out
which was the right way. We had no
clue. The sound of the sea, it is true, had
grown faint in our ears, so that we were
further inland; but excepting for the dyke
which I had crossed after my meeting with
the tramps, we had no landmark to tell us
where we were.

Harrod thought he remembered the dyke,
but how far it was from the high-road that
we wished to reach we could neither of us
exactly determine. The tract of country
was a little beyond our usual beat, or we
should have been less at a loss. But there
was no sign or sound yet of the market-town
through or by which we must pass before we
reached our own piece of marsh-land.

There was no doubt about it that we were
lost on the marsh, and all that we could do
was to jolt slowly along, avoiding dykes
and unseen pitfalls, and waiting quietly for
the day to show us our whereabouts. Luckily in these midsummer nights the hours
betwixt dusk and dawn are but short. Only

Harrod seemed to be concerned about it.
He kept asking me whether I was warm ; he
kept begging me not to give up and go
to sleep. I suppose he was afraid of the fever
for me. But, for my own part, I felt no in-
convenience. I was not cold, and I had no
more inclination to go to sleep.

I do not remember that we talked of anything in particular,—I do not remember that
we talked much at all. I think I was afraid
to speak—I think I was afraid that even he
should speak—the silence was too wonderful,
and the vague sense of something unspoken,
unguessed, was sweeter than any words.
It was the deepest silence I have ever felt :
there wasn't so much as the sound of a bird,
or of a stirring leaf, or of the breath of the
sleeping cattle,—even the gentle moaning of
the sea was hushed now in the distance. It
was as though we two were alone in the
world.

Sometimes I could see that smile of Mr
Harrod's flash out even in the darkness as
he would turn and ask if I was quite warm ;
and sometimes he would merely bend over me
and wrap the rug—tenderly, I fancied—more

closely around me. Ah, it was a midsummer night's dream! But at last nature was
stronger than inclination—I was young and
healthy—and I dropped asleep. When I
awoke, a promise of coming light was in
the east, the sea was tremulous with it, and
long purple streaks lined the horizon. Overhead the sky was fair, although the thick
white fog still lay in one vast sheet all
around us. Out of it rose the market-town
straight before us, dark and sombre from
the shining sea of mist.

We were trotting now along the beaten
track towards it, and Mr Harrod was urging
on the weary mare with one hand while
the other was round my waist. The gig was
narrow for two persons, and I suppose I
should have risked being thrown out in my
unconscious state if he had not done so.
He took away his arm as soon as I stirred,
and I shook myself and looked at him.
Had my head been resting on his shoulder?
and if it had, why was I so little disturbed?

"I am afraid I have been asleep," said I.

"Yes," answered Mr Harrod, "you have
been asleep. I hadn't the heart to rouse

you again, you were so tired. But we shall
soon be at home now."

"Why, we have got back into the track!"
I exclaimed.

"Yes," laughed he. "When the town
began to appear through the mist, it was a
landmark to me, though I believe I tumbled
over the path at last by a mere chance."

He said no more. We were soon out
into the high-road again, and climbing the
street of the town. We were the only stirring people in it, and this made me feel more
conscious of my strange adventure than all
the hours that I had spent alone on the
marsh with my companion.

For the first time I began to wonder what
mother would say. Once out of the town, we
sped silently along the straight familiar road
that led towards our own village. The mist
was beginning slowly, very slowly, to clear
away, and the hills upon which our farm
stood loomed out of it in the distance. In
the marsh on either side of us the cattle
began to stir like their own ghosts in the
white vapour, and gazed at us across the
dykes with wondering, sleepy eyes.

The stars were all dead, and above the
mist the quiet sky spread a panoply of steely
blue, while out above the sea the purple
streaks had turned to silver, and sent rays
upwards into the great dome. Hung like a
curtain across the gates of some wonderful
world unseen, a rosy radiance spread from
the bosom of the ocean far into the downy
clouds above that so tenderly covered the
naked blue—a radiance that every moment
was more and more marvellously illumined
by that mysterious inward fire, whose even
distant being could tip every hill and moun-
tain of cloud-land with a lining of molten gold.
Unconsciously my gaze clung to the spot
where a warmth so far-reaching sprung from
so dainty a border-land of opal colouring ; and
when at last the great flame was born of the
sea's grey breast, I felt the tears come into
my eyes, I don't know why, and a little sigh
of content rose from my heart. I was tired,
for the sunrise had never brought tears to
my eyes before.

"I hope you'll be none the worse," said
Harrod, glancing at me uneasily, and urging
the horse with voice and hand; "but I'm

afraid your parents will have been sadly anxious anyhow."

Alas! I had not thought of it again. I sat silent, watching where the familiar solid curves of the fortress upon the marsh began to take shape out of the fog.

"If I hadn't met you I should have been out on yonder marsh now," I said.

I thought he would have said something about being glad he had met me, but he did not. He only answered, "I ought not to have allowed you to fall asleep."

I laughed at that. "If it had not been for you, I should be asleep now on that bank where I first heard you," I declared. "And I should have got my death of ague by this time, I suppose."

Still he said nothing. There was some misgiving on his mind which no words of mine removed. I felt it instinctively. Even when I said—and as I write it down now, I marvel how I *could* have said it—even when I said softly, "Well, I regret nothing; I have enjoyed myself," he did not reply.

I wondered at it just for a moment, but no mood of his could damp my complete

content. Even though, as I neared home,
I began to be more and more uneasy about
my parents' anxiety, no cloud could rest on
the horizon of this fair, sweet dawn of day.
I could not see beyond the barrier of that
ever-widening, ever-brightening curtain of
glorious light, — but there it was, making
glad for the coming of the blessed sun that
would soon fill the whole space of heaven's
free and perfect purity.

The coldness of the sky and of all the
world was slowly throbbing with the waken-
ing warmth. What was there beyond that
burning edge of the world, beyond that sea
of strange exultant brightness?

We began to climb the hill, and on the
garden terrace stood my father. He was
waiting for me just as he had waited for me
on that night in May when he had told me
to be friends with Trayton Harrod.

CHAPTER XXIII.

MOTHER never scolded me at all for my adventure, and of course I was much more sorry than I should have been if she had done so.

As I stood there in the cool grey dawn, with my wet habit, the dew-drops still standing on the curls of my red hair, my face— I make no doubt—pale with distress, and my grey eyes at their darkest from the same cause, I suppose I looked rather a sorry spectacle, and one that melted her heart. Anyhow, I know that she put her arm round me and gave me a hasty kiss before she pushed me forward to meet father. For a moment I felt something rise in my throat, and I suppose I ought by rights to have cried. But I did not cry. I was too happy in spite of it all, and luckily neither father

nor mother were of those people who expect
one to cry because one is sorry.

As I have said, they neither of them uttered
a word of rebuke. I gave my explanation,
and it was accepted. Father only declared
that it was a very good thing Trayton Harrod
had met me when he did; and mother only
remarked that "least said soonest mended."
I suppose they were both glad to have me
safe home. And that drive with father's
bailiff, which had meant so much to me, was
thus buried in sacred silence.

It was the day that Joyce was to come
home. As I dressed myself again after the
couple of hours' sleep which I could not
manage to do without, I remembered that
it was the day for Joyce to come home.
How was it that I had not thought of it?
How was it that I had not thought of it
all yesterday, nor for many yesterdays before it?

I was conscious that even my letters to
my sister had been fewer and more hurried
than they were at the beginning of her
absence. I was angry with myself for it,
for I would not have believed that any

length of absence could have made her anything but the first person of importance in my life. But of course, now that she was home again, everything would be as before.

I felt very happy to think that I was to see her again. I begged the gig to go down to the station and meet her myself : the mare was used to me now, so that even Joyce would not be nervous. Her face lit up with her own quiet smile as she saw me, breaking the curves of the sweet mouth, and depressing, ever so little, that short upper lip of hers, that always looked as if it had been pinched into its pretty pout. She looked handsomer than ever. I don't know whether it was because it was so long since I had seen her, but I thought she was far more beautiful than I had ever imagined. I pitied poor Frank more than ever for having to wait so long for a sight of her.

"Why, Meg," said she, as she came out with all her little parcels, "how tanned you are. I declare your hair and your face are just upon one colour."

I laughed aloud merrily.

"Well, if my face is the colour of my hair,

it must be flame indeed," I cried. " But
I've been out haymaking, you see, all the
time that you, lazy thing, have been getting
a white skin cooped up in a London parlour.
Oh, my dear! I wouldn't have been you."

" No, you wouldn't have liked it," answered she. " I was pleased to be of use to
poor old aunt, but it was rather dull, and
I must say I'm glad to be home."

" Everybody has missed you dreadfully,"
said I. " As for mother and Deb, they
can't tell me often enough that I'm not able
to hold a candle to you."

" Oh, what nonsense, Meg!" murmured she;
" you know well enough they don't mean it."

" My dear, I don't mind," cried I. " I
know it well enough, and I can do my own
bit of work in my own way all the same.
But mother has missed you, and no mistake,"
added I, " though as likely as not she won't
let you guess it. She wanted you home
long ago, only then Captain Forrester came
down again."

A troubled shade came over Joyce's face,
as I had noticed it come once or twice before, at mention of her lover's name.

"He came down for a few days a week ago, you know," I added. "I told you so, didn't I?" I was not quite sure whether I had even remembered to give that great piece of news.

"Oh yes, you told me," replied Joyce in a low voice.

"He inquired a great deal after you, of course," I went on. "He asked me to give you a great many messages."

She did not answer. A blush had crept up on her dainty cheek, as it was so apt to do. But we had reached the hill, and I jumped down and walked up it, giving her the reins to hold. And when we got to the top, Deborah was there hanging clothes in the back-garden ready to catch the first sight of us along the road, and Reuben at the gate looking half asleep because he had been out the best part of the night with Jack Barnstaple searching for me in the fog. There was no time for any more private talk.

Mother, it is true, did not come to the gate, that not being her way; and when we got inside, you might have thought Joyce had been no farther than to market from the way in which she received her. But that meant nothing, it was only Maliphant manners; and father said no more than—" You're looking hearty, child," before he took me away to write out his prospectus for him, because his hand was stiff.

It was not till late evening that I got time to have a chat with Joyce in the dear old attic bedroom that she and I had always shared, and I was anxious for a chat. She had brought back two new gowns for us, and apart from all I had to say to her, I wanted to see the new gowns. I had never cared for clothes till quite lately. I used to be rather ashamed of a new frock, as though folk must think me a fool for wearing it, and had been altogether painfully wanting in the innocent vanity which is supposed to be one of a young girl's charms. But lately it had been different. I wanted to look nice, and I had my own ideas of how that was to be achieved. Alas! when I saw the gowns, I knew that they did not meet my views.

Joyce was settling her things, — laying aside her few laces and ribbons with tender care. She opened the heavy old oak press

and took out the gowns with pride.   I think
that she was so busy shaking them out that
she did not see my face; I hope so, for I
know it fell.   The gowns were pale - blue
merino—the very thing for her dainty loveliness, but not, I felt instinctively, the thing
for a rough ruddy colt like me.

"Won't they spot," said I diffidently.

"That's what mother said," replied she, a
little sadly; "but, dear me, they're our only
best frocks,—we shan't wear them o' bad
weather."

I am so glad I said no more, for she had
brought me a book from London—it was a
novel by a famous author of whom we had
heard : the author was a woman, and I had
expressed a great wish to read it in consequence.   I was very pleased to think that
Joyce should have remembered it.   I recollect that I kissed her for it, and I thought
no more about the frocks,—I only felt that
it was nice to have sister home.   I had not
known until now how much I had missed
her.

"I wonder how we shall all get on when
you go away for good and marry that young

man of yours," said I. " It don't seem as if
the place were itself somehow when you are
not there."

" Time enough to think of that when the
day comes," answered Joyce, I thought a
trifle sadly.

"Well, yes, may be," said I doubtfully;
"and yet it isn't so very far off, you know.
And if only you had a little more determination in you, it might be a great deal nearer."

" You seem to be very anxious to get rid
of me just as soon as you have got me
home," said she, with just the merest tone
of wounded sensibility in her voice.

Of course I laughed at that — it wasn't
really worth answering. But I could have
said that since three weeks ago, I had
learned that which made me think it harder
than ever that Joyce should be separated
from the man she loved. I had not thought
much of her or her concerns of late, but
now that she was close to me I felt very
sorry for her. When Joyce had gone away,
I had been conscious of a curious feeling of
inferiority with regard to her, as though she
knew some secret which was to me sealed ;

but now—now I felt that there was a rent in the cloud that divided us, I felt that I could look into her world, I felt that I was on her level. And it was only with a more delicate feeling of sympathy than formerly that I began to give her some of the messages with which Frank had entrusted me.

I could not exactly pretend that he had looked very miserable, but I could assure her of his continued ardent devotion to her, and this I did most fervently. Somehow, when I had entered upon this task, I began to feel that it was rather a queer compliment to assure a girl that her lover was not forgetting her, and I asked myself why I felt obliged to do it?

She listened quietly to all that I repeated to her of the short interview; but when I began to speak of my endeavours to induce mother to cut the term of the engagement short, she interrupted me with that serene air of determination which I knew there was no gainsaying

"Meg," she said, "I want you never to do that again. I want you to understand once and for all that if things don't come naturally,

it's because I believe that they oughtn't to
come at all.   If Frank cares for me as he
says, he will care for me just as much at the
end of a year, and I had rather wait and see."

I looked at her open-mouthed.

" I think you're a queer girl," I said at
last.   " I shouldn't have thought you wanted
to punish yourself for the sake of putting a
man to a test.   But I suppose I don't understand.   That's the sort of way mother talks,
and I know it's very wise, and all that; but,
dear me, I think it's all stuff wanting to sit
down and wait till the wave comes over you.
I'm sure that if *I* wanted a thing very badly,
I should love to fight for it—I should *have*
to fight for it."

Joyce sighed a little sigh, and sat down by
the window looking out into the deepening
twilight.

It was close upon midsummer, and the
evenings were exquisitely long and luminous,
the twilight stretching almost across to the
dawn.   After the heat of the day, lovely
soft grey mists rose in transparent sheets
off the marsh below us, and floated upward
towards the hill.   It was not a thick fog

as it had been the night before, but just a
ghostly veil thrown across the land, above
which lights twinkled amid dark houses on
the distant hill.   There was not a breath
of wind, and in the silence the lapping of
the sea came faintly to our ear.   Joyce
looked out into the mist.

"Of course," continued I after a while,
"I'm not engaged to a man, and so I don't
know what I should do if I were."

"I think you would do what you do in
other matters," answered Joyce.   "I think
you would try very hard to get your own
way.   But then you and I are not alike."

No, we were not alike, I felt that.   And
I supposed that my sister was right, and
that the only difference lay in my being
more obstinate.

"I don't think that a woman ought to
fight to have her own way," added she in
a low voice.

I considered a moment before I understood what she meant.   "Do you mean to
say that if any one fights, it ought to be
the man?" asked I.   "Well, you *are* an unreasonable girl!   Good gracious me!   When

Frank lifts a finger you are angry with him."

Joyce smiled a faint smile like the grey mists below.

"I don't think you know *what* you mean nor *what* you want," added I impatiently.

Without taking any notice of my short tone, she said gravely, "I know that it will be all as it is ordained."

When Joyce talked about things being as they were ordained, it always put me in a horrible temper; and it was either this or some little feeling of awkwardness in my mind about Harrod, which made me reply very shortly when she began asking me presently about the new bailiff.

From some motive entirely incomprehensible to myself, there arose within me a sudden dislike to the idea that Joyce should guess at my liking for him. And so when she asked what he was like, I replied gruffly, "Oh, like many other men—plain and very obstinate."

This was true, but the impression that I gave in saying it was false. I knew that perfectly well, but I was too proud to

change it, although in my heart I felt
ashamed that I should be guilty of any
sort of deception towards my dear simple
Joyce, and when I was really so glad to
have her back again.

She looked distressed for a moment, but
then she brightened up and said gaily,
"Well, many a good fellow is plain ; and
as for being obstinate, that should be to
your liking."

"So it is," said I.   "Of course."

"I hope father and he get on nicely.   I
hope he isn't obstinate with father."

I laughed.   "Oh, birds of a feather, you
know," said I.   We're all obstinate together.
But we none of us waste words, so we get
on first-rate."

Joyce sighed a little.   "Mother said what
a good fellow he was, but father wouldn't
say a word about him to me," she said.
"Of course he never does.   But I don't
think he's looking well.   He has aged so
of late."

I looked at her defiantly.   So many
people had said the same thing during the
last few months.

" Good gracious ! Joyce," I cried. " You're always saying that. Father's hale and hearty enough. Folk are bound to grow older. And I can tell you one thing, he's not half so touchy as he was. He and Squire haven't had more than two rows since you left. That's a very good sign."

" Yes, I *am* glad of that," agreed Joyce. " The Squire's too good a friend to quarrel with. And though of course I know the quarrels never meant anything, they used to make me uncomfortable, Meg, and worse than ever when you used to follow father's way. It didn't seem pretty in one of us girls, dear. Something's good for mere manners. We don't think enough of them."

I was silent. My manners were certainly of the worst when my heart did not go with them. But I was conscious that I was not quite the same girl as I had been when my sister left. Even to the Squire I was different : since his talk to me on the garden terrace I had felt no inclination to be anything but gentle to him.

" Of course, if father quarrels with the bailiff it's as bad for his own health as if he quarrelled with the Squire," went on my sister concernedly.

"Why, dear me, Joyce, who said he quarrelled with him?" cried I. "I only said they were both obstinate. Father wouldn't think of quarrelling with his bailiff."

I took off my dress and hung it up, and shook out my red mop of hair before I said another word.

Then I added, "And I think Mr Harrod is very considerate towards father. "He's far too good a fellow not to be respectful to an old man." I felt bound to say that much for honesty.

"Well, then you do like him?" cried Joyce.

"Who said I didn't?" answered I. "He's a downright honest fellow, with no nonsense about him."

It wasn't quite what I felt about Trayton Harrod, but it was as near as I could get to the truth, and it seemed to give Joyce some idea of my liking him, for she turned round with a brightened face, and laid her hand on my shoulder.

"O Meg, you can't think how pleased

you make me by saying that," she murmured softly. "I have been afraid you
would just set your face against the poor
man out of mere obstinacy, and make
things unpleasant for everybody. You do
sometimes, you know. And when you
never mentioned him in your letters, I
made sure that was the reason. I thought
you were just making yourself as disagreeable as ever you could, to show you hated
his coming to Knellestone."

"Well, you must think me a dreadful old
cross-patch," laughed I awkwardly.

"You *are* tetchy when you have a mind
to be, you know, though you can be so
bright when you're pleased that one's forced
to love you. That's just the pity."

"Well, of course, I *did* hate a bailiff coming to Knellestone," answered I. "But now
that I see how much cleverer he is about
farming than we are, I'm pleased."

"I see," said Joyce. "Then he *is* clever?"

"Oh yes," answered I. "He's clever."

Joyce paused.

"Well, then," she said diffidently, "I hope
before long you'll be real good friends. I

have often thought, Meg, that the folk here aren't bright enough for you. I believe if you weren't set down in a country village, you'd be a real clever girl."

I laughed, not ill pleased.

"Oh no, Joyce," said I. "I expect what you and I think clever wouldn't really be so."

"I know more than you think," said Joyce sagely, nodding her pretty head with an authoritative air. "I don't mean book-learning clever, I mean mother-wit. And do you know, Meg, I do so hope that Mr Harrod being here may make a difference to you. But you don't seem to have seen much of him yet."

"Oh yes," said I evasively. "He comes in to supper most nights; and of course one meets outdoors now and then in a country place."

"Well," concluded Joyce, with a sort of air of resignation, "of course it wasn't to be expected you'd be great friends just at once. It's a great deal to be thankful for you don't quarrel."

"Oh no," said I; "we don't quarrel."

And then we both said our prayers and got into bed.

But for a long while I lay awake thinking why I had pretended that I did not like the new bailiff, and whether I really was a clever girl ; and—shall I confess it ?— hoping a little that the pale-blue dress would become me. And then, as I fell asleep, and far into my dreams, the memory of my ride with Trayton Harrod shone through the mist, and I thought again of that bar of silver promise across the dawn beyond which I had not been able to see.

CHAPTER XXIV.

Two whole days passed without Mr Harrod coming to the Grange. I daresay nobody else noticed it; I daresay *I* should not have noticed it if—if I had not thought that he would come to inquire how I did after our adventure. I was always supposed to resent being asked how I did: and here I was, quite hurt because a young man whom I had known not three months had omitted to do so!

I took covert means of finding out that father and Reuben had seen him, and that he was well; and I am quite sure that I blushed with pleasure when, on the morning of the third day, mother said that she was certain the white curtains at " The Elms " must be getting soiled, and suggested that I should carry up a new pair. Harrod was

becoming quite a favourite with her, or she
would never have taken so much trouble
for his comforts,—it was no necessary duty
on her part. I blushed, but I did not think
that any one had noticed it.

When mother had left the kitchen, however, with the key of the linen-press, I saw
that two little black eyes were fixed on me
with a merry twinkle. They made me angry
for a moment, I don't know why, but it was
a shame to be angry with old Deb, especially
when her dear old red face was so kindly
and affectionate : it was not always wont
to be so.

"Well, well, I'm glad to see folk are for
forgiving that poor young man for being
bailiff at Knellestone," said she, with good-
humoured banter. "When I see'd what a
fine masterful chap it were, I had my doubts
it 'ud end that way."

"What way, if you please ?" asked I
haughtily.

Deborah laughed. "What do you say,
Joyce ?" said she, turning to my sister, who
was intent upon some one of the household
duties that she was so glad to be back at.

"They aren't quite so hard on the young man as they were for going to be, are they?"

"I don't quite understand," said Joyce, with perfectly genuine innocence. "Why should mother be hard upon him? It isn't his fault if he's father's bailiff. Besides, I'm sure mother sees how useful he is to father."

Deb laughed louder than ever. "There, bless you, my dear," said she, "you never could see round a corner; but you've more common-sense than the lot of 'em. Why should folk owe the man a grudge, to be sure? All the same, your mother 'll spoil him afore she's done with him. Curtains, indeed! I never knowed a bailiff as needed 'em before."

Mother came back at that moment with the things, and I hastened to beg Joyce to accompany me up to "The Elms" after dinner. Somehow, although in my heart I knew that I was longing to see Trayton Harrod again, a sudden shyness had come over me at the thought of meeting him, and I wanted Joyce to be there.

Joyce, however, would not come: she begged off on the score of many household

jobs that had got behindhand in her absence, and mother said that I might just
as well go alone and get the thing done
with Dorcas's help, for that of course the
bailiff was sure to be out at that time of
day.

So alone I was forced to go. Most likely,
as mother said, Mr Harrod would be out, but
I took Taff with me : a dog was better than
most human beings, and with Taff at my
heels I felt my self-consciousness evaporate.

I crossed the lane and skirted the brow of
the hill behind the pine-tree lane : the mill
arms faced the village with a west wind, but
the breeze had dropped since morning, and
the air was heavy and thunderous. I thought
I would go round by the new reservoir and
see how the work was getting on. Mr
Harrod would very likely be there : it was
that one among his new ventures about
which at the moment he was the most
excited, and the pipes were just about to
be laid. Even if I met him, he was not
obliged to know that I was going to " The
Elms."

My heart began to beat a little as I drew

near the group, but the bailiff was not there; only old Luck, the sheep-dog, ambled towards me wagging his tail, and I knew that Reuben could not be far off. Sure enough, there he was among the men who were just leaving off work, talking to Jack Barnstaple.

"I want to know whatever he needs to come stuffing his newfangled notions down folks' throats as have thriven on the old ones all their lives?" the latter was saying. "We don't understand such things hereabouts. We haven't been so well brought up. He'd best let us alone."

"Yes, I told him so," said Reuben sagely, shaking his stately white head, that looked for all the world like parson's when he had his hat off; "but these young folks they must always be thinking they knows better than them as has a life's experience. But look 'ere, lads, we han't been educated at the Agricultural College at Ashford, ye know."

"Blow the Agricultural College," muttered Jack Barnstaple.

"Yes; and so he'll say when he finds out he's none so sure about these Golding 'ops. And so master 'll say when he finds as he's dropped all his money over pipes and wells as was never meant to answer."

" What do you mean by that, Reuben ? " said I, coming up behind him. And I am sure that my cheeks were red, and my eyes black, as father would declare they were when the devil got into me. " What was never meant to answer ? "

Reuben looked crestfallen, for of course I know he had not expected me to be within hearing, and the other men began to pack up their tools for going home.

" Well, miss, it don't stand to reason that a man can expect water to go up hill to please him," said Reuben, with a grim smile.

" Water finds its own level, Reuben," explained I, sagaciously ; " Mr Harrod told me that, and father said so too. The spring is on yonder hill, and if the pipes are laid through the valley to this hill, the water is bound to come to the same level."

I saw a smile upon the faces of the men, and Reuben shook his head.

" There's nothing will bring water up hill saving a pump, miss," said Jack Barnstaple,

gloomily: he always said everything gloomily,—it was a way he had.

"Nay," added Reuben, looking at me with
those pathetic eyes of his that seemed to say
so much that he can never have intended;
"it may be a man or it may be a beast, but
some one has got to draw the water up hill
afore it'll come. It may run down yonder
hill, but it won't run up this 'un of its own
self. 'Taint in nature."

"Well, Reuben, I advise you to keep to
talking of what you can understand," said I
crossly. "I should have thought you would
have had sense enough to know that Mr
Harrod must needs know better than
you."

A faint provoking smile spread over Reuben's lips. "Young folks holds together,"
said he laconically. "''Tis in nature."

I flashed an angry glance at the old man,
but I saw a lurking smile—for the first time
in my experience—on the face of stolid Jack
Barnstaple, who had lingered behind the
others. My face went red, as red as my red
hair, and I stooped down to caress the dog.
What did the man mean? what had Deb

meant that morning in the kitchen? But I raised my head defiantly.

"Well, I think you had just best all of you wait and see," said I severely. "You'll feel great fools when you find you have made a mistake."

I was alluding to the water scheme; but it struck me afterwards that the men might have misunderstood me. But it was too late to correct the mistake, and without another word I ran down the hill to the path that led to "The Elms."

My cheeks were hot with the consciousness that I had a secret that could be guessed even by Reuben Ruck; the consciousness made my heart beat again very fast. But it need not have done so: as was to have been expected, Mr Harrod was not at home.

Dorcas and I put up the curtains together, and then I was left alone in the little parlour while she went to make me a cup of tea. It was the first time I had been alone in that room—his room.

A bare, comfortless, countryman's and bachelor's room, but more interesting to

me than the daintiest lady's parlour.   By
the empty hearth, the high-backed wooden
chair in which he·sat; beside the wide old-
fashioned grate, the hob upon which sang the
kettle for his lonely breakfast; in the centre
of the rough brick floor, the large square
oaken table at which he ate; on the high
chimney-piece, the pipes that he smoked,
the tobacco-jar from which he filled them,
a revolver, and an almanac; on the walls,
two water-colour drawings, one represent-
ing an old gentleman in an arm-chair, the
other the outside of a country house over-
grown with wistaria; standing in the corner,
a handsome fowling-piece, which I had seen
him carry; in the bookshelf between the
windows, the books that he read.

I wandered up and looked at them : a curious assemblage of shabby volumes, although
at that time they embodied to me all that
was highest in culture.   That was ten years
ago, and I was in love.   Had it not been so,
I might have remembered that father's library was at least as good.

Milton, a twelve-volumed edition of Shakespeare, a Bible, a Pilgrim's Progress, a vol-

ume of Cowper's Poems, a volume of Percy's Reliques, Adam Smith's Wealth of Nations, Chaucer's Canterbury Tales, Sir Walter Scott's Novels, Byron, Burns, some odd volumes of Dickens, and then books on Agriculture, the authors and their titles strange to me,—this is all I remember. A mixed collection — probably the result of several generations, but not a bad one if Trayton Harrod read it all and read it well.

I looked at it sadly. Save the Walter Scott novels, the Burns's poems, the Bible, and the Pilgrim's Progress, I knew none of them excepting by name, and not all of them even then. I felt very ignorant, and very much ashamed of myself. For I never doubted but that Harrod read and knew all these books, and how could a man who knew so much have anything in common with a girl who knew so little ? I resolved to read, to learn, to grow clever. Joyce had said that I was clever—Joyce might know ; why not ?

I took the volume of Milton down and sat upon the low window-seat reading it. It was rather dreadful to be immediately confronted with Satan as an orator, for I had

never been used to consider him as a person-
age, but rather as a grim embodiment of evil
too horrible to be named aloud. But the rich
and sonorous flow of the splendid verse fascinated me, and I read on although I didn't
understand much that I read.

My thoughts wandered often to notice that
the square of carpet was threadbare, and
that I must persuade mother to get a new
one; or to gaze out of the window upon the
sloping bosom of the downs whereon this
house stood lonely—a mark for all the winds
of heaven : in the screne solitude the sleepy
sheep strayed idly, cropping as they went—
white blots upon the yellow pastures. And
all the while I was listening for a footstep
that I feared yet hoped would come, longing
to be away and yet incapable of the determination which should take me from that chance
of a possible meeting. But, long as I have
taken to tell it, the time that I waited was
not ten minutes before a heavy foot made
the boards creak in the passage and a hand
was on the door-knob. I started up, my
cheeks a-flame—the volume of Milton on
the floor. But when the door opened it

was Squire Broderick who stood in the opening. I don't think the red in my face faded, for I was vexed that he should see me there, and I fancied that he looked surprised.

"Oh, do you know if Harrod is at home?" asked he.

"No, he's not," answered I, glancing up at the clean windows; "and I've been putting up fresh curtains meanwhile."

"They look delicious," said the Squire, with a little awkward laugh, not quite so hearty as usual. "What care you take of him!"

"Mother is a dreadful fidget, you know," murmured I.

"And at the same time you took a turn at Harrod's library," smiled he, picking up the volume which lay near my foot. "Milton! Rather a heavy order for a child like you, isn't it?"

I flushed up angrily. A child!

"Do you understand it?" asked he.

I struggled for a moment between pride and truthfulness. "No," said I, "not all. Do you?"

He smiled,—that kind, sweet smile that made me ashamed of being cross.

"Come, I'm not going to confess my ignorance to you," he laughed. "I'm too old," and he took hold of my arm to help it into the sleeve of my jacket, which I was trying to put on.

But at that moment Dorcas brought in the tea, and of course I was obliged to stay and have some, and even to hand a cup to the Squire to please her : country folk stand on ceremony over such things, and I did not want to offend Dorcas.

"You'll step in to-night and see Joyce, won't you?" said I, for want of something to say, for I felt more than usually awkward. "She looks better than ever. She hasn't lost her country looks."

"I am glad of that," said he, glancing at me, although of course he must have been thinking of sister; "they're the only ones worth having." And then, although he promised to come in and welcome her home, he went back to our first subject of talk.

"As you're so fond of reading, you ought to get hold of a bit of Shakespeare," said he.

"Should I like that?" asked I. "I like poetry when it sounds nice, but I like the Waverley novels best."

"But Shakespeare is novel and poetry too," said the Squire. "I'm no great reader of anything but the news myself, but I like my Shakespeare now and again."

"Father keeps all those nice-bound books in the glass case," said I, "and I don't believe mother would let *me* have them."

The Squire laughed. "Your mother thinks girls have something better to do than to read books," smiled he. "Reading is for lonely bachelors like Trayton Harrod."

"He's no more lonely than you are, Mr Broderick," said I, — "and yet you always seem to be quite happy."

He did not answer, and I was sorry for my thoughtless words, remembering that brief episode in his life when he had not been lonely.

"So you think I am always quite happy?" said he at last.

I blushed. Somehow the question was of a more intimate kind than the Squire had

ever addressed to me before, for although
he had spoken familiarly to me on my
account, he had never allowed me to know
any feeling of his own. I was afraid he
must be going to speak to me about Joyce.

"Oh yes," I replied lightly; "I think
you're one of the jolliest people I know."

"Well, you're right, so I am," said he
gaily; "and I'm blessed in having rare good
friends. But it does sometimes occur to me
to think that I am pretty well alone in the
world, Miss Margaret."

He looked round at me in his frank way,
but I noticed that the hand which held his
stout walking - stick trembled a little. I
blushed again. It was very unusual for
me, but he made me feel uncomfortable.
I did not want him to tell me of his love
for my sister, for I felt that, if he did, I
must tell him of her secret engagement to
his nephew, and that would be breaking
my promise to my parents. Suddenly an
idea struck me : I thought I would take the
bull by the horns.

"You should marry," said I boldly.

He looked at me in blank astonishment.

"Of course," added I, "there's no one hereabouts that would be good enough for you—unless it might be Mary Thorne, and she is only a manufacturer's daughter. You must have a real lady, of course. You should go and spend a bit of time up in London, and bring back a nice wife with you. Wouldn't it brighten up the country-side!"

I marvel at myself for my boldness. I, scarcely more than a child, as he had said, to a man so much older than myself! But the Squire did not seem in the least offended, only he looked very grave.

"You don't approve of people not marrying in what is called their own rank of life, I see," he said presently, with a twinkle of humour in his eye.

"No," said I gravely; "I agree with father."

"Ah!" said the Squire, with the air of a man who is getting proof of something that he has affirmed. "I told Frank so the other day. As a rule the farmer class consider it just as great a disadvantage to mate with us as we do to mate with them."

I bit my lip. So he did consider it a fall-

ing down for a gentleman to marry a farmer's
daughter! Well, let him just keep himself
to himself then. But what business had he
to go meddling with Frank's opinions? I
was very angry with him.

"I think you're quite right," I said shortly.
"They do."

"It takes a very great attachment to bridge
over the ditch," said he meditatively.

There came a time when I remembered
those words of his, but at the moment I
scarcely noticed them. I thought I heard
a footstep on the gravel without, and my
fear of being surprised by the master of the
house came back stronger than ever, because
of the presence of the Squire.

"I must be getting home now," said I
hastily. "I'm afraid there's a storm coming
up;" and even as I spoke, a deep low growl
echoed round the hills.

The Squire fully agreed that there was
no time to be lost if one did not want to
get a drenching, and on the slope outside
we parted company, he promising once
more to come up in the evening and see
Joyce.

The bailiff was not within sight. I had got over my visit quite safely; but, alas! I am not sure that I was relieved. I walked homewards as fast as I could, for heavy drops had begun to fall, and flashes of light rent the purple horizon. The sun had set, leaving a dull red lake of fire in the cleft, as it were, of two purple-black cloud-mountains; above the lake a tongue of cloud, lurid with the after-glow, swooped like a vulture upon the land, where every shape of hill and homestead and church spire lay clearly defined, and yet all covered as if with a pall of deathly gloom.

The storm advanced with terrible swiftness. By the time I had crossed the hop-gardens and was climbing the opposite lane, it had burst with all its strength, and was tearing the sky with seams of fire, and emptying spouts of rain upon the land. I was not afraid of a storm, but certainly I had never seen a fiercer one.

I ran on, forgetful for the moment of everything but the desire to be home, and thus it was that I did not notice footsteps behind until they were alongside of me, and

Mr Harrod's voice was saying almost in my ear, " Miss Maliphant!"

The voice made me start, but the tone of it sent a thrill through me.

"I should have thought that one piece of foolhardiness was enough for one week," added he, with a certain look of feeling, veiled under roughness, that always seemed to me to transform his face.

"I took no harm from the other night," said I.

"Well, you may thank your stars that you didn't," answered he; "and you certainly will get wet through now."

I laughed contentedly. " *That* won't hurt me," I said. " I've been up at ' The Elms ' to put up fresh curtains." I hadn't meant to tell him, but a sudden spirit of mischief, and I don't know what sort of desire to see the effect of the speech on him, prompted me.

" To ' The Elms '!" cried he in a disappointed tone. And then in a lower voice— " to put up the curtains for me?"

- " Yes," answered I demurely; "mother sent me."

What he would have answered to that I

don't know, for at that moment the sky seemed suddenly to open and to be the mouth of a flaming furnace full of fire, far into the depths of the heavens : it was the hour that should have been twilight, but it was dark, save when that great sheet of blue light wrapped the marsh in splendour; then the brown and white cattle huddled in groups on the pastures, the heavy, grey citadel on the plain, the wide stretch of sea that, save for the white plumes of its waves, was ink beyond the brown of its shallows, the wide stretch of monotonous, level land, the rising hill, with the old city gate close before us,— all was suddenly revealed in one vivid pano- rama, and faded again into mystery. The thunder followed close upon the lightning— a deafening crash overhead.

"By Jove !" said Harrod. "That's close. I hope you're not frightened of a storm."

"Frightened !" repeated I scornfully.

"Some girls are," said he half apologeti- cally, looking at me with admiration.

"Not I, though," I laughed.

But as I spoke my heart stood still. We had climbed the hill and had reached a spot where the trees overshadowed the road, nearly meeting overhead; a fiery fork crossed the white path in front of us, there was a kind of crackle in the wood, and a blue flame seemed to dart out of the branch of an elm close at hand.

"Great God!" ejaculated Trayton Harrod under his breath, and he flung his arm around me and dragged me to the other side of the path.

I had said an instant before that I was not frightened, and I had spoken the truth; but if I had said now that I was not frightened it would have been because the sweet sense of protecting strength, which this danger had called forth, had brought with it a happiness stronger than fear.

"Can you run?" said he. "We must get away from these trees."

I could not speak, something was in my throat, but I obeyed him. We ran till we reached the Abbey, where it stood in the great open space of its own graveyard, and there we drew aside under the shadow of the eastern buttress, protected a little by the projecting arch.

" You're wet through," said he, laying his hand upon my arm."

I laughed again, not in the sort of exultant way I had laughed when he had asked me if I was afraid of lightning, but in a low, foolish kind of fashion.

" It won't hurt me," murmured I. " Nothing hurts me. I'm so strong."

" Oh yes, you're the right sort, I know," said he ; "but all the same, you ought to have stayed at ' The Elms ' till it was over. If I had been there I should have made you stay."

How angry those words would have made me a week ago ! But now they thrilled me with delight, and with that same tender fear and longing of fresh experience that had haunted me ever since the night upon the garden cliff. Could he really have " made " me do anything ?

" I shouldn't have stopped," I said ; " no, not for any one. I'm not afraid of a storm." But I think there was very little of my old defiance in the tone. He laughed gently, and I added: " I don't see any use in waiting here."

I advanced forward into the open, but as
I did so, a fresh flash rent the clouds and
illumined the ground all about us, revealing
darkest corners in its searching light.   He
took me by the hand and drew me once
more into the shadow—not only into the
shadow of the buttress this time, but of the
ruined roof of a transept, where only the
lightning could have discovered us.

" Not yet," he said gently ; and although
there was no need for it, he still held my
hand in his.

My foolish heart began to beat wildly.
What did it mean ?   Was that coming to
pass about which I had wondered sometimes
of late ?   I wanted to get away, and yet I
could not have moved for worlds.   I waited
with my heart beating against my side.

But he did not speak, he only held my
hand in his firmly, and I felt as though his
eyes were upon me in the dark.   I may
have been wrong, but I felt as though his
eyes were upon me.

All at once in the ivied wall above our
heads an owl shrieked.   We started asun-
der, and I felt almost as though I must

have been doing something wrong, so hard did my heart thump against my side.

"Fancy that poor old barn owl being able to frighten two sensible people," laughed Trayton Harrod. "But upon my word I never heard him make such a noise before."

I made no reply. I came out once more into the path, and, turning, held out my hand.

"The storm is over," I said. "Good night."

"Oh, I must see you home," said he. "It's getting quite dark."

He walked forward with me, but the spell was broken, only my heart still beat against my side.

"You'll come in to supper?" said I, when we reached the gate. I felt myself speaking as one in a dream. The only thing that I was conscious of was a strange and foolish longing that he should not go away from me.

He did not answer for a moment, but then he said: "I'm afraid I mustn't. I'm drenched through,—I shouldn't be presentable."

I had forgotten it : we were, in truth, neither of us presentable.

"Well, you must come to-morrow," said I, in as matter-of-fact a tone as I could muster. "Mother expects you, and my sister is home now."

He stepped forward in front of me and opened the front door, which always stood on the latch. The brightness from within dazzled me for a moment as he stood aside to let me pass, and there in the brightness stood Joyce.

How well I remember it! She had on a soft, white muslin dress, that fell in straight, soft folds to her feet, and made her look very tall and slender, very fair and white. The light from the lamp fell down on her shining golden hair; her blue eyes were just raised under the dark lashes—gentle and serene. Suddenly, for the first time in my life, there flashed upon me a sense of the contrast between myself and her.

I stood there an instant in my dripping old brown frock looking at her. Then I turned round to introduce Mr Harrod. But the house door had closed behind me again. He was gone.

CHAPTER XXV.

TRAYTON HARROD did come to supper the next day.

I remember that mother upbraided him for having been so many days absent, and that he made some kind of an excuse for himself; and I remember that I blushed as he made it, and felt quite awkward when he shook hands with me and asked if I had taken any cold of the night before. But I was happy — very, very happy. I was happy even in fancying that I saw a certain self-consciousness in him also, in the persistence with which he talked to mother, and in something that crossed his face when our eyes met, which was almost as often as his were not fixed on Joyce, where she sat in her old place by the window.

Every one always was struck with Joyce

at first, and I had been so anxious that Harrod should duly admire her that I had purposely refrained from saying much to raise his expectations, so that no doubt his surprise was as great as his admiration; and I had never seen my sister look handsomer than she did that night.

There was a little increased air of dignity about her since she had been to London and had been thrown a little more on her own resources, which sat with a pretty style upon her serene and modest loveliness. She looked people in the face as she never used to do, raising her eyes without lifting that little head of hers that was always just slightly bent, like some regal lily or drooping tulip. She talked a little more, and she blushed seldomer.

She did not talk much to Mr Harrod, but then he was very busy explaining his scheme of water-supply to Mr Hoad, who had dropped in to supper. But she talked quite brightly to Squire Broderick when he came, as he had promised, to bid her welcome home, and shone in her very best light, just as I had wished she should shine —the beautiful hostess of our home.

It was a happy evening, typical of our happy home life, that, flecked as it may have been by little troubles, as the summer sky is flecked with clouds, was yet fair and warm as the bright July days that followed one another so radiantly.

Ah me, how little I guessed that night that there were not many more such happy family parties in store for us when we should sit around that board united and without a gap in the family circle! It is good that we cannot see into the future. No gathering cloud disquieted me that night—no fears for myself nor for any of those whom I loved : I was absorbed in that one throbbing, all-engrossing dream which was slowly beginning to fill my life.

Absorbed, yet not quite so much absorbed but that I could feel sorry for my sister's sake that one who had been there was now absent : where Frank Forrester had been, Trayton Harrod now was. I could not honestly say to myself that I wished it differently, but I was sorry for Joyce. She, however, did not seem to be depressed—she was very bright; the gladness she had in

being at home again gave her beauty just
that touch of sparkle which it sometimes
lacked.

It was a warm evening, and when supper
was over we drew our chairs around the low
porch that led on to the lawn, and took our
ease in the half light. It was very rarely
that we sat thus idle, but sometimes, of
summer evenings, mother was fond of a bit
of leisure herself, and she never made us
work when she was idle. The scent of the
sweet-peas and the roses came heavy upon
the air; the dusk was still luminous with
lingering daylight, or with heralding a moon
that had not yet risen.

"I hear you have got Southdowns into
your flock, Harrod," said the Squire. "I
hope you won't have any difficulty with
them. I feel confident they ought to do,
but when I tried the experiment it certainly
failed."

"Perhaps they weren't carefully looked
after," answered Harrod. "Of course you
have got to acclimatise animals just as well
as people, and the more carefully the more
delicate they are."

"Ah, I daresay it may be a matter of management," agreed the Squire. "I hadn't a very good shepherd at the time."

"I don't leave it to a shepherd," said Harrod. "Shepherds are clever enough, and there are plenty of things I learn from them and think no shame of it; but they know only what experience has taught them, and these shepherds have no experience of Southdowns. Besides they are a prejudiced lot, and they set their faces against new ventures."

The Squire laughed, a laugh in which Mr Hoad—subdued as he always was by Mr Broderick's presence—ventured to join.

"Yes, you're right there," he said. "You get it hot and strong, I daresay, all round. They snigger at you pretty well in the village for this water-scheme of yours, I can tell you, Mr Bailiff."

My cheek flamed, and Mr Hoad went down one step lower still in my estimation.

"I daresay," said Harrod shortly, and he said it in a tone of voice as much as to say, "and I don't care."

"But it's a very clever thing, isn't it?"

asked dear old mother, in her gentle voice.
" I never could have believed such a thing
was possible."

I could have said that Reuben declared
it was not possible, but I would not have
told on Reuben for worlds.

" It's not a new discovery," answered the
Squire, who had taken no notice of the solicitor, and took mother's question to himself,
"but it's a very useful one."

" I wonder you haven't thought of using
it before for the Manor," put in father.
"You must need a deal of water there."

I felt a glow of satisfaction at seeing
father stand up for Harrod; for as far as
I knew anything of their discussions, I
had fancied he was not very keen upon the
scheme.

" I had thought of it," answered Mr
Broderick; "but I didn't think I could
afford it. I didn't think it would pay for
one individual."

I fancied father was vexed at this.

He began tapping his foot in the old
irritable way which I had not noticed in
him of late, for, as I had remarked to Joyce

on her return, I thought he was far less peppery than he used to be, and I fancied it was a good sign for his health.

"Neither do we think it will pay for one individual," said he. "We intend to make many individuals pay for it."

He said "we," and I was pleased.

"Well, of course I shall have the water laid on to the Manor, and am grateful to the man who started the thing," said the Squire in a conciliatory tone; "but I'm a little doubtful as to your making a good job of it all round. Marshlands folk are very obstinate and old-fashioned."

"Oh, they'll come to see which side their bread's buttered on in the long-run," declared Harrod confidently.

But Mr Hoad smiled a sardonic smile, and the Squire added : "I'm afraid it will cost you a good bit of money meanwhile, Maliphant. However, as I sincerely hope you are going to make your fortune over these new hop-fields, it won't signify." It was, to say the least of it, an indiscreet speech, not to say an unallowable one; for I believe there is nothing a man dislikes so

much as having his affairs talked of in public.
It was not at all like the Squire, and I could
not help thinking, even at the time, that
Harrod must have in some way nettled Mr
Broderick, although I was very far from
guessing at the cause of the annoyance.

Father rose and walked slowly down to the
edge of the cliff.   I could not tell whether
he did it to keep his temper or to conceal
his trouble, for I fancied he looked troubled
as he passed me.

" The hops are a splendid crop now," said
Harrod, without moving, as he lighted a fresh
pipe.   He never allowed himself to show if
he were vexed.

But the Squire did not reply.   He rose
and followed father.   I'm sure he was sorry
for what he had said.   It was the solicitor
who answered.

" It ought to be a fine crop," he said.
" Maliphant paid a long price for it."

" How do you know what price he paid
for it ? " asked Harrod sharply.

I fancied Mr Hoad looked disconcerted
for a moment, but he soon recovered himself.

" Well, to tell the truth, he did me the

honour to ask my advice," he replied, with a sort of smile that I longed to shake him for. "No offence to you, Mr Harrod, I hope," he added blandly. "I know Maliphant holds your opinion in the highest reverence, but—well, I'm an old friend."

My blood boiled in the most absurd way; but Harrod was far too wise to be annoyed, or at any rate to show it. He only remained perfectly silent, smoking his pipe.

Father and the Squire came up the lawn again; I wondered what they had said to one another. The evening was fresh and fragrant after the rain of the night before upon the hot earth; the dusky plain lay calm beneath us; the moon had just risen and lit the sea faintly in the distance; nature was quiet and sweet, but I felt somehow as though the pleasure of our evening was a little spoilt. Mother tried to pick up the talk again, but she was not altogether lucky in her choice of subjects.

"Why, Squire, the girls tell me the right-of-way is closed across that bit of common by Dead Man's Lane," said she. "Do you know whose doing it is?"

Father turned round sharply.

"It never was of much use," said Mr
Hoad, answering instead. "The way
by the lane is nearly as short, and much
cooler."

"It depends where people are going,
whether it is as short," said father. "It's
a flagrant piece of injustice. Do you know
who's to blame for it?"

Mr Hoad looked uneasy, and did not reply; and the Squire burst into a loud laugh.

"Why, the Radical candidate, to be sure,"
said he, with a pardonable sneer in his hearty
voice. "Those are the men for that kind
of job."

"Mr Thorne!" exclaimed mother. "No,
never!"

"Ay," said father under his breath; "a
man who can rob his fellow-creatures in big
things, won't think much of robbing them in
little things!"

"You shouldn't run down your own party,
Maliphant," laughed the Squire. "Thorne
is no particular friend of mine, but robbery
is too big a word."

"I understand he's a very charitable man,"

said mother, who always would have fair play.

"Yes," echoed Joyce. "You don't know, father, what a deal of good Mary Thorne does among the poor."

Father rose; he was trembling. I saw a fire leap in his eye.

"It's easy to give back with your left hand half of what you robbed with your right," said he in a low voice, that yet resounded like the murmur of distant thunder; "but it isn't what those who are struggling for freedom will care to see in their representative."

"Oh, I don't believe in a Radical party, here anyhow," said the Squire abruptly,— "not even if you began to back the candidate, Maliphant."

"I shall not back the candidate," said father grimly.

"No," laughed the Squire. "He has done for himself with you over this right-of-way."

"When I see a man who declares he is going into Parliament on the people's side, deliberately try to rob the people of their

lawful possessions, I feel more than ever that
the name of Radical is but a snare," said
father.

His face had grown purple with emotion;
his voice quivered with it; his hand shook.

I saw mother look at him anxiously, and
I saw a sullen expression settle down upon
Mr Hoad's detested face.

"Now, Laban, don't go getting yourself
into a heat," said mother, in her quiet, sensible voice. "You know how bad it is for
your health, and it's unpleasant for all parties
besides."

"I can't make head or tail of the Radicals
myself," began the Squire, who, it must be
remembered, spoke ten years ago. But
mother interrupted him.

"Come, come, Squire," said she, in the
pretty familiar way in which she always addressed him, "we'll have no more politics.
The girls and me don't understand such talk,
and it isn't civil to be leaving us o' one side
all the evening."

He laughed, and asked what we wanted
to talk about, and at the same time Mr
Hoad came forward to take his leave.

He smiled, shaking hands with mother, but his smile was a sour one, and I noticed that he scarcely touched father's hand.

"I suppose Hoad is in a bad temper because you won't take up Thorne's cause," said the Squire, as soon as the solicitor had passed up the passage.

Father gave a grunt of acquiescence, and the Squire turned to us with most marked and laudable intent to obey mother. and change the talk.

"Have you heard the news?" he asked. "Young Squire Ingram is to be married to Miss Upjohn. I heard it yesterday riding round that way."

Mother looked up eagerly. The subject was one quite to her own mind, but the news was startling.

"Never to Nance Upjohn of Bredemere Farm?" asked she.

"The very same, Mrs Maliphant," replied the Squire. "Folk say they are to be married at Michaelmas."

"Heart alive!" ejaculated mother, lapsing into the vernacular in her excitement. "Isn't old Squire in a fine way?"

"I believe he doesn't like it," agreed Mr Broderick evasively.

"Why not, pray?" asked father, rousing from his reverie.

I always noticed that once he had been brought to arms upon the real interest of his life, he was the more ready to take fire upon secondary subjects even remotely connected with it. No one answered him, and he repeated his question.

"Why not, pray? The Upjohns come of as good a stock as we do, though they haven't been so long upon the soil."

"To be sure," put in mother quickly. "And I've been told she's as well schooled as any town miss. I don't mean to say she isn't good enough for the young Squire, only I've heard say the old gentleman is so terribly particular."

"Yes, indeed, she's as well behaved and pretty a young woman as you could find anywhere," declared Mr Broderick warmly. "Old Ingram can have no objection on anything but the score of connection."

"Connection? What's that?" exclaimed father. "If the girl comes of a different stock to the lad, why must it needs be of a worse one? Faith, if I were neighbour Upjohn, 'tis I would have the objection."

"Nonsense, Laban," said mother, half annoyed.

"No; I wouldn't let any girl of mine wed where it was made a favour to receive her," continued father hotly.

"There are plenty among the gentry, too, that would make it no favour at all to receive a nice young woman just because she came of another class," added mother, with a vexed manner. "There's good honest folk all the world over, and bad ones too."

"Right you are, old woman," answered father, after a moment's hesitation, with generous repentance. "There's some among them that I'm proud to shake by the hand. But all the same, a prejudice is a prejudice, and a class is a class."

"You'd best come indoors," said mother, still annoyed. "It's getting chill, and you've been out too long already, I believe."

He rose with the habit of obedience, and we all stood up, but he tottered as he walked.

I saw Harrod, who was beside him, stretch out his arm.

He did not take it; he walked in bravely, the others following—all but myself and the Squire. I saw he was troubled,—I saw he wanted to speak to me, and I did not like to move.

"Your father is so emphatic, so very emphatic," he murmured; "but I hope, Miss Margaret, that you do not misunderstand me."

I looked at him a little surprised. I could not see how it could signify to him whether I misunderstood him or not. If it had been Joyce, it would have been different.

"Oh no, I don't misunderstand you," said I, a little hurriedly, for I wanted to get indoors. "It was quite clear."

I was vexed with the Squire. I was angry with him for having seemed to make light of Harrod's knowledge and of Harrod's schemes. I thought it was not fair of him before father — and when he had always bidden me fight the bailiff's battles for the good of the farm. So I answered a little proudly: "You can't grumble if father and

I have our pride of class as well as you yours."

"No, I don't grumble," said he, with a smile, and yet I fancied with something half like a sigh too. "Only I, personally, have very little pride of class."

"I'm glad to hear it," said I. And I ran indoors.

I wanted to say good night to Trayton Harrod. But in the parlour there was nobody but my sister leaning up against the open casement and looking out into the fragrant summer night.

"What are you doing?" I asked abruptly. "Where are they all?" And as I spoke I heard a step die away on the gravel outside.

"I have just let Mr Harrod out," answered she, "and I came to close up the windows. I think mother has gone upstairs with father. I don't believe he is well."

I did not answer. It was Joyce's place again, now that she was home, to close the front door after the guests. But it was the first time that Harrod had left the Grange without bidding me good night. When

Joyce asked me where the Squire was, I
did not care. It was she who hastened out
to meet him and made mother's apologies,
—it was she who let him out as she had let
out the bailiff.

It needed a sudden scare about my dear
father to bring me back to myself. He had
had a bad fainting fit—the worst we had ever
seen him in. It was the bell ringing up-
stairs, and mother's frightened voice calling,
that waked me from a dream. And the
evening ended badly, as I had had a silly
presentiment that it would end.

CHAPTER XXVI.

THE next morning the sun shone, and the world was as gay as ever. Father declared himself well and hearty; complained of no pain, and betrayed no weakness—was merry at the breakfast-table over a letter of Frank Forrester's, and withdrew with it as usual to his study, where he spent more and more time opposite the portrait of Camille Lambert, and left farm matters more and more to his bailiff.

For me the sun shone the more brightly because of a short delightful ten minutes with Trayton Harrod, in which we said nothing in particular, but that chased away the tiny shadow of disappointment that had crossed the horizon of my sweet, dawning experience, and banished it—disgraced and ashamed—into oblivion.

It was a very short ten minutes. Miss
Farnham and the Vicar's wife had been to
call, and the Hoad girls had come to ask us
to go to a ball at the Town Hall. "Oh,
do come," they had said, "and bring the
bailiff;" and my dignity had flamed into my
cheek, and I had been grateful to mother for
promptly refusing for us, and even to old
Miss Farnham for declaring that we were
more sensible than most girls, and weren't
always on the watch for new occasions to
pinch in our waists. Miss Farnham, I recollect, had declared afterwards that it was
only a dodge to catch father.

It was after the guests had left, and while
we were waiting for mother to get her
bonnet on for a drive, that Harrod and I
got those short ten minutes to ourselves.

Joyce had gone to Guestling to lunch with
some friends, and mother had proposed to
Harrod to drive us over to fetch her, so that
at the same time she might look at a cow
which he had found for her there for sale.

We set forth, Harrod driving mother in
the cart with the steady old black horse, and
I riding Marigold alongside.

I saw as soon as we set out that he was just a little shade out of spirits. It troubled me at first, but I soon guessed, or thought I guessed, what it was about.

"Wasn't that Mr Hoad I saw up a-top of the hill with you and Laban?" asked mother, just after we had set out.

Harrod nodded.

"Whatever does the man want meddling with farming?" asked mother. "I shouldn't have thought he was a wiseacre on such like."

Harrod shrugged his shoulders; he evidently didn't intend to commit himself.

"Mr Hoad wouldn't wait to hear if other folk thought him a wiseacre before he'd think he had a right to interfere," laughed I. "Those smart daughters of his came inviting Joyce and me to a ball just now."

"You're not going?" asked Harrod quickly.

"No, no," answered mother. "I don't hold with that kind of amusement for young folk. There's too many strangers."

"Why don't you want us to go?" asked I softly.

He didn't reply; he whipped up the horse a little instead.

"Miss Farnham declared our going would have been made use of to try and draw father into the election against his will," said I. "But she's always got some queer notion in her head."

"Well, upon my word, I don't believe there's much these electioneering chaps would stick at," declared Harrod contemptuously. "I declare I believe they'd step into a man's house and get his own chairs and tables to go against him if they could."

Mother laughed, but Harrod did not laugh.

"And if they can't have their way, there's nothing they wouldn't do to spite a fellow," added he.

"Why, whatever has Mr Hoad been doing to spite you?" asked mother.

"Nothing, ma'am, nothing at all," declared the bailiff. "There's nothing he could do to spite me, for I don't set enough store by him, and I should doubt if there's any would be led far by the words of a man that shows himself such a time-server."

He spoke so bitterly that I looked at him in sheer astonishment.

"I thought Mr Hoad seemed to have taken quite a fancy to you last night," said mother.

Harrod laughed harshly.

"Yes," he said; and then he added abruptly, "there's some folk's seemings that aren't to be trusted. They depend upon what they can get."

"Good gracious!" said mother. "Whatever could Mr Hoad want to get of you?"

"Excuse me, ma'am, I don't know that he wanted to get anything," declared Harrod, evidently feeling that he had gone too far. "I know no ill of the man. I don't like him—that's all."

Mother was silent, but I said boldly, "No more do I."

And there talk on the subject ended. It was not until many a long day afterwards that I knew that Hoad—moved, I suppose, by Harrod's argument against father on the previous evening—had tried to persuade him to help in some sort against his employer in the coming political struggle. He little knew the

man with whom he had to deal, and that no
depreciatory remarks which spite might induce him to make to father upon his farming
capacities would have any influence upon
father's bailiff.   Only I was glad I had
agreed with him in not liking Mr Hoad.   It
got me a reproving look from mother, but it
got me a little smile from him, which, in the
state of my feelings, added one little grain
more to the growing sum of my unconfessed
happiness.

It was a long way to Guestling.   A way past
" The Elms " and its hop-gardens, and many
other hop-gardens again, where the bines
were growing tall and rich with their pale
green clusters; away between blackberry
and bryony hedges that the stately fox-
glove adorned, between banks white with
hemlock; away on to the breast of the
breezy downs, where the hills were blue
for a border, and solitary clumps of pines
grew unexpectedly by the roadside.

The west became a sea of flame beyond
the vastness of that swelling bosom, just as
it had been almost every evening through
that glorious summer, and set a line of blood-

red upon the horizon for miles around, firing
clots of cloud that floated upon lakes of tender
green, and hemming other masses with rims
of gold that were as the edges of burning
linings to their softness.

Mother was almost afraid of it.   She declared that she had never seen a sunset that
swallowed up half the heavens like that, and
she wondered what it boded ; for even after
we had turned and left the west behind us,
the clouds that sailed the blue were red with
it still.

When we got near to Guestling we were
overtaken by Squire Broderick on his roan
cob. .I think he had intended to ride farther,
but he seemed so delighted to find mother
out of doors, that he could not detach himself from our party.

"Why, Mrs Maliphant," I remember him
saying, with that half respectful, half affectionate air of familiarity that he always used
to our mother, "if you knew how becoming
that white bonnet is, you would put it on
oftener.   It's quite a treat to see you out
driving."

Mother declared that only business had

brought her out now; and I remember how
the Squire told her she would never find a
new friend to take the place of an old one,
not if Harrod were to find her a cow with
twice the good points of poor old Betsy.
And while Mr Broderick was paying sweet
compliments to mother, Harrod and I ex-
changed a few more of those common-place
words, the memory of which made me merry
even when presently I was obliged to
drop behind and ride alongside of the
Squire.

I had something to say to him, and as it
related to the bailiff, I was not unwilling to
drop behind. The night before he had made
light of those schemes and improvements on
the farm of which I was beginning to be so
proud, and I had not thought it fair of him
to try and set his own *protégé* in a poor light
before father. I meant to tell him so, and
this was the opportunity.

" Mr Broderick," said I, driving boldly
into my subject, " why did you talk last night
as if things were going badly on the farm ?
You told me a while ago that all the farm
wanted was a younger head and heart upon

it,—somebody more ambitious to work for it.
Yet now, one would almost fancy you mistrusted the very man you recommended, and
wanted to make father mistrust him."

I saw the Squire start and look at me—
look at me in a sharp, inquiring sort of way.

" I did not intend to give that impression,"
he said.

" Well, then, you did," said I, wisely
shaking my head. " Any one could have
seen it. You were quite cool about the
water-scheme. Why, father took his part
against you."

" I think you exaggerate, Miss Margaret,"
murmured he.

" Oh no, I don't," I insisted. " And if
I am rude, I beg your pardon ; but I think
it a pity you should undo all the work I have
been doing. Besides," added I, in a lower
voice, " it's not fair. You said you were
' afraid ' he was spending too much money,
and you ' hoped ' he would make a fortune
over the hops. It didn't sound as if you
believed it would be so."

" Well, so I do hope a fortune will be
made," smiled he.

"Ah! but you said it as if it might have been quite the contrary," insisted I.

"Did I ?" repeated he humbly.

"Yes," declared I. "If you don't think Mr Harrod manages well, you should tell him so; you are his friend."

The Squire was silent—moodily silent.

"Ah, who can tell what is good management in hops!" sighed he at last. "The most gambling thing that a man can touch. All chance. Twelve hours' storm, a few scalding hot days, and a few night-mists at the wrong moment, may ruin the most brilliant hopes of weeks. I have seen fortunes lost over hops. A field that will bring forth hundreds one year, will scarcely pay for the picking the next. No man ought to touch hops who has not plenty of money at his back."

"Do you think father knows that hops are such a tremendous risk ?" I asked.

"Oh, of course he must know it," answered the Squire.

And there he stopped short. I did not choose to ask any more. It seemed like mistrusting father to ask questions about his affairs. But I wondered whether he was a man who had "plenty of money at his back."

"I think Harrod is a safe fellow, and a clever fellow," added the Squire. "A cool-headed, hard-headed sort of chap, who ought not to be over-sanguine though he is young."

The words were not enthusiastic, they were said rather as a duty,—they offended me.

"Oh, I am sure you would not have re-commended him to father unless you had had a high opinion of him," said I haughtily. "And I am glad to say that father has a high opinion of him himself, and always follows his advice. I do not suppose that anything that any one said would prejudice father against Mr Harrod now. In fact, we all have the highest opinion of him."

With that I touched Marigold with the whip, and sent her capering forward on to the cart. Mother started, and reproved me sharply; but at that moment we drew up at the farm gates, and she turned round to beg the Squire would spare her a few minutes to give his opinion also upon the contemplated purchase. Harrod looked round, and I was angry, for she had no right to have done it. I do not know how the Squire could have consented, but he did so, though half unwillingly, and demurring to Harrod's first right.

" The Squire is such a very old friend of ours," I murmured, half apologetically, to the bailiff on the first opportunity. " Mother has so often asked his advice."

" Yes, yes, I quite understand," replied he. And then he added—I almost wondered why—" I suppose you remember him ever since you were a child ? "

" Oh yes," laughed I ; " he used to play with us when we were little girls, and he was a young man."

" A young man !" smiled Harrod. " What is he now ? "

" I should think he must be nearly thirty-five," said I gravely. " And you know he's a widower."

" Indeed ! Well he's not too old to marry again," smiled Trayton Harrod, looking at me.

" That's what mother says," answered I. And then I added—and heaven knows what induced me to do it, for I had no right to speak of it—" some folk think he's sweet on my sister."

It was unlike me to babble of family secrets. I glanced at my companion. There was a little scowl upon his brow; it was usually there when he was thinking, and he was ruffled still with vexation at mother's unusual want of tact. He looked after her where she was talking with the Squire.

" Oh, is it to be a match?" he asked carelessly.

"Oh, dear no," laughed I. "Joyce——"

I was going to say "Joyce cares for some-one else," but luckily I remembered that solemn promise to mother just in time.

"Joyce doesn't even think he likes her," I added instead.

He turned to me and broke into a little laugh. I thought it almost rude of him, and wondered whether he, too, thought that a farmer's daughter was not worthy of marriage with a Squire.

But he was looking at me—he was looking at me with a strange look in his eyes. Yes, there was no mistaking it—it was a look of admiration, a look of almost tender admir-

ation, and as I felt it upon me, a blush rose
to my cheek that so rarely blushed, and the
power of thinking went from me ; I only felt
his presence.

I don't know how long we stood thus; I
suppose it was only seconds before he said,
" I believe you would put that sister of yours
before you in everything, Miss Margaret."

I made an effort to understand him, for I
think I was in a dream.

" Yes, she's so beautiful ! " I murmured.

" Beautiful ! " echoed he.

There was something in the tone of his
voice that made me lift my eyes to his
face.   His gaze was fixed on the gate of the
farmyard.   I followed his gaze.   Joyce had
entered, and was coming towards us.   This
was where we had arranged to meet.

She shook hands with Harrod and then
with the Squire, who joined us with mother :
we all went together into the cow-shed.

I don't remember what remarks were
made upon Betsy's proposed successor,—I
don't even remember if we bought her or not.
I don't think I was in the mood to attend
much to the matter.   I was roused from a

brown study by a curious remark of Trayton Harrod's.

Mother had found occasion to ask him whether the woman whom she had provided for him at " The Elms " made him comfortable, and was pleasant-spoken. It had been on her mind, I know, ever since he had been there.

" She does her work," answered the bailiff. " I don't know if she's pleasant-spoken. I never speak to her."

" That's not the way to get the best out of a woman," laughed the Squire. " We poor bachelors need something more than bare duty out of our servants." He said it merrily, and yet I did not think he was merry.

" I want no more than duty," repeated Harrod. " Talking, unless you have something to say, is waste of time."

" You'll have to mend your manners, my lad, if ever you hope to persuade any young lady to become your wife," laughed the Squire again.

" I never should hope to do any such thing," answered Harrod. " I shouldn't be

such a fool." And with that he walked
away out of the farmyard and began untying
the cart for the homeward journey.

Mother looked after him, puzzled for a
moment. Then, nodding her head at the
Squire, she said softly, "Ah, that's what all
you young men say till you've fixed on the
girl you want. You're none so backward
then."

I fancied the Squire looked a little uncomfortable, but he said lightly, "Do you
think not, Mrs Maliphant? Well, nothing
venture, nothing have, they say. Harrod
has had his fingers burnt, I suppose. A bit
sore on the subject. But he'll get over it.
He's a nice lad; though, to take his word
for it, his wife wouldn't have a very cheerful life of it!"

"Well, we needn't take his word for it,"
said the mother. "And, good gracious me!
it's fools indeed that would want to wed
upon nothing but sugar. There'd be no grit
in love at all if we hadn't some duties towards one another that weren't all pleasant.
'Tis in the doing of them that love grows
stronger. I've always thought you can't

smell the best of roses till you get near enough to feel the thorns."

This speech of mother's comes back to me vividly now, but at the time I was scarcely conscious of it.

Trayton Harrod's words, "I shouldn't be such a fool," were ringing in my ears. What did he mean by them? I looked round after him and saw that my sister had strolled across to where he was waiting by the cart. It was natural enough—it was time to be getting homewards. But as I looked I saw him bend towards her just a little and say something. The expression of his face had softened again, and the scowl on his sunburnt brow had faded, but his lips were pressed together so that they were quite thin instead of full as they appeared in their normal shape, and I wondered why he looked so, and why what he said made the blush, that was now so much rarer than it used to be, creep up Joyce's cheek till it overspread her fair brow and tipped her delicate little ears with red.

An uncontrollable, unreasonable fit of anger took possession of me. I flew across

the yard to that corner where Marigold was
tied beside the dog-cart.

"I suppose you read a great deal of evenings?" Joyce was saying.

And Harrod answered shortly, "No, I
don't so much as I used to do. I am too
much taken up with other things."

Simple words enough, but they set my
heart aflame, yet left me sick and sore.

I undid the mare with a rough hand, and,
before she had time to see what I was about,
I set my foot in the stirrup and sprang into
the saddle. She was used to my doing that,
but she was not used to my doing it in that
way.

She reared and kicked. My thoughts were
elsewhere, and it served me right that, for
the first time in my life, she threw me.

I heard a scream from mother, and the
next moment I felt that a man's arm had
helped me up from the ground.

I was not hurt, only a little stunned, and
when I saw that it was Trayton Harrod who
had picked me up, I broke away from him
and staggered forward to mother.

"I'm not hurt, mother, not a bit," said I,

and then I burst into tears. Oh, how ashamed I was!— I who prided myself on self-control.

But she put her arm round me and laid my head on her shoulder, and her rare tenderness soothed me as nothing else in the world could have done. I kept my face hid on her neck, as I had done when I was a little child, and used to be quite confident that she could cure every wound.

Yet it was only for a moment.

" I had better ride and lead the mare," I heard the Squire say in a low, concerned voice. " She won't be fit to mount again, or even to drive the cart."

I lifted my head.

" Oh, indeed, Squire Broderick, I'm not in the least hurt," said I, as cheerfully as I could, for I was grateful for those kindly tones. " I can ride Marigold home perfectly well."

" No, my dear, that you won't," said mother, all her decision returning now that her alarm was over. " I've had quite enough of this fright for one day."

Joyce returned from the farm with a glass

of water and Harrod by her side with some
brandy that he had begged at the doctor's
house hard by.   I drank the water but I refused the brandy, and scoffed at the notion
of the doctor coming out in person.   Then I
got into the cart.   I insisted on driving, and
as the horse was the quiet old black Dobbin,
mother consented.   Joyce sat behind, and
Harrod rode after upon Marigold.

The Squire showed signs of joining our
caravan at first, but as I turned round and
assured him once more that I was perfectly
well and begged him to continue his road,
he was almost obliged to turn his horse back
again in the direction in which he had been
going when he overtook us.   But he still
looked so very much concerned that I was
forced to laugh at him.   I think it was the
only time I laughed that day.

The drive home was soothing enough
across those miles of serene pasture-land
whose marge the sea was always kissing,
and where the sheep cropped, in sleepy
passiveness, beneath faint rosy clouds that
lay motionless upon the soft blue; the vast
dreamy pastures, browning with autumn tints

of many planes of autumn grasses that
changed as they swayed in the lazy breeze,
were hemmed by a winding strip of beach,
pink or blue, according as the sun was behind
or above one, and to-night bordered beyond
it by a stretch of golden sand, over which
rows upon rows of little waves rippled with
the incoming tide. We drove along the
margin of the beach; the yellow sea-poppies
bloomed amid their pale, blue-green leaves
upon every mound of shingle, and not even
the distant church-spires and masts of ships,
that told of man's presence, could disturb the
breathless placidity that no memory of storm
or strife seemed to awaken into a throb of
life.

But suddenly upon the vast line of wide
horizon, where the sea melted into the sky
with a little hovering streak of haze, a throb
of light stirred : at first it was but a spot of
gold upon the bosom of the distance, but it
was a spot that grew larger, though with a
soft and rayless radiance unlike the dazzle of
the sun-setting; then out of the breast of
it was made a red ball that sent a path of
gilded crimson down the sea, and tipped the

crest of every little wave that crept towards us with a crown of opalescent light. It was the sun's last kiss welcoming the moon as she rose out of the sea.

It was a rare and a beautiful sight, and to me, who loved the world in which I lived so well, it should have brought joyousness. And yet it did not please me. I would rather have had it chill and stormy, with a thick fog creeping up out of the sea—a fog such as that through which Trayton Harrod's tall figure had loomed the first time that I had met him just on this very tract of land.

CHAPTER XXVII.

On the day following I met Frank Forrester in the lane by the Vicarage.

I verily believe I had forgotten all about him during the past few days, but that very morning I had remembered that he was most likely at the Priory for that garden-party to which father had so annoyingly forbidden us to go; and I vowed in my heart that, by hook or by crook, my sister should see him before he left the neighbourhood. It was a regular piece of good luck my meeting him thus, but I thought, when he first saw me, that he was going to avoid me. He seemed, however, to think better of it, and came striding towards me, swaying his tall, lithe body, and welcoming me even from a distance with the pleasant smile, without which one would scarcely have known his handsome face. I was glad he had thought better of it, for I should certainly not have allowed him to pass me.

"Holloa, Miss Margaret," said he, when we were within ear-shot, "this is delightful. I was afraid I shouldn't get a chance of seeing any of you, as I am forbidden the house. How are you?"

"I am very well," said I, looking at him.

I fancied he had grown smarter in his appearance than he used to be; there was nothing that I could take hold of, and yet somehow he seemed to me to be changed.

"Why weren't you at the garden-party yesterday?" asked he. "It was quite gay."

"Yesterday? Was it yesterday?" said I, half disappointed. "We weren't allowed to go, you know. We wanted to go very much."

He looked at me in that open-eyed way of his for a moment, and then he shifted his glance away from my face and laughed a little uneasily.

"Was I the cause?" he asked.

"Oh, dear no," cried I eagerly, although in my heart I knew well enough that, with mother, he had been. "But you know father never did like the Thornes. They belong to that class that he dislikes so. What do you call it—capitalists ? Why, he hates them ever so much worse than landed proprietors, and they are bad enough."

I said this jokingly, feeling that, as of course Frank sympathised with all these views and convictions of father's, he would understand, even though he might not himself feel just as strongly towards those members of the obnoxious class who had been his friends from his youth upwards. But a shadow of annoyance or uneasiness — I did not know which—passed over his face like a little summer cloud, although the full, changeful mouth still kept its smile.

"And Mr Thorne has done something special to vex him," I continued. "He has closed the right-of-way over the common by Dead Man's Lane. So now father has forbidden us to go to the house."

The slightest possible touch of scorn curled Frank's lip under the silky brown moustache.

"That's a pity," said he.

"Well," said I, "you would feel just the same, of course, if these people didn't happen to be old friends of yours, and they never were friends of father's. He disliked them buying the property from the very first."

"It makes things rather uncomfortable to drive a theory as far as that," laughed Frank.

Of course it was what I often felt myself, but somehow it vexed me to hear him say so. If he was the friend to father that he seemed to be, he had no business to say it, and specially to me.

"Well, anyhow it's the reason we didn't go to the garden-party," said I shortly. And then I repeated again, and in a pleasanter tone, "But we wanted to go very much, of course."

"Ah yes," answered he, glancing at me and then away again; and referring, I suppose, to the pronoun I had used, "Your sister is home again now. Of course I heard it in the village. What a pity you couldn't come. We had a dance afterwards —altogether a delightful evening, and you would have enjoyed it immensely. Besides," he began, and then stopped, and then ended abruptly, "every one missed you."

I laughed. "That means to say every one missed Joyce," I said. "I am not so silly as to think people mean me when they mean Joyce—some people, of course, more particularly than others."

It was rather a foolish remark, and he took no notice of it.

"Your sister is well? I hope," was all he said.

"Oh yes, she's well," I answered.

And then there was an awkward pause. I wondered why in the world he did not ask any of the innumerable questions that must be in his mind about her, and yet I felt that it was natural he should be awkward—natural that he should not want to talk to me about her.

I did not know exactly what to say, and yet I would not let this golden opportunity slip.

"You must come and see for yourself," said I boldly, without in the least considering what this course of action lay me open to from mother. "She's prettier and sweeter

than ever, Joyce is, since she's been to
London."

He turned quickly and looked at me with
his widest gaze.

" Come and see her ! Why, Miss Margaret,
you know that's impossible !" ejaculated he.

" You came to see us the last time you
were in Marshlands," said I. " You don't
come to see Joyce—you come to see father.
Father would be dreadfully hurt to think you
were in Marshlands and didn't see him.   He
doesn't know you are here."   This was true,
but whether father would have wished me to
run so against mother's wishes, I did not stop
to think.

" Your sister was not at home when last
I came to the Grange," said he softly.

I almost stamped my foot with vexation
at the lack of recklessness in this lover of
Joyce's, whose ardent devotion I had begun
by envying her once upon a time.   But I
reflected that it was both foolish and unfair
to be vexed, because Frank Forrester was
only keeping to the word of his agreement.

" You come to see father, not to see
Joyce," I repeated dogmatically.   " Father

doesn't seem to be happy about the way that notion of his is turning out."

" That notion ? " repeated the young man in an inquiring tone of voice.

I looked at him.

" Yes," said I.   " I don't know exactly what it is, but something or other that father and you have got up between yourselves."

Still he looked puzzled.

" Some school, or something for poor children," explained I, I think a trifle impatiently.

" Oh, of course, of course," cried Frank. " I didn't quite understand what you were referring to, and one has so many of those things on hand, so many sad cases, there is so much to be done.   But I remember all about it.   We must push it.   It's a fine scheme, but it will need a great deal of pushing, a great deal of interest.   It's not the kind of thing that will float in a day. Your father, of course, is apt to be over-sanguine."

I did not answer.   It crossed my mind vaguely that three months ago it had been father who had said that Frank was apt to be over-sanguine; or rather, who had given it so to be understood, in words spoken with a kindly smile and some sort of an expression of praise for the ardour of youth. " It's to the young ones that we must look to fly high," he had said, or words to that effect.

" Well, you must come and talk it over with father," said I, somewhat puzzled. " He thinks a great deal of you."

" Ah! And so do I think a great deal of him, I assure you," cried Frank. " He's a delightful old man! So bright and fresh and full of enthusiasm. One would never believe he had lived all his life in a place like this, looking after cows and sheep. There are very few men of better position who can talk as he talks."

I suppose I ought to have been pleased at this, but instead of that it made me unaccountably angry for a moment. I thought it a great liberty on the part of a young fellow like Captain Forrester to speak like that of an old man like my father. But one could not be exactly angry with Frank. In the first place, he was so pleasant, and good-natured, and sympathetic, that one felt the fault must be on one's own side ; and then it would have been waste of time, for he would either never have perceived it, or he would have been so surprised that one would have been ashamed to continue it.

However, I tried to speak in an off-hand way as I said : " Yes, he doesn't often get any one here whom he cares to talk to, so of course he is very glad of whoever it is that will look at things a bit as he does." And then, afraid lest I should have said too much, and prevent him from coming to the Grange after all, I added, " But he's really fond of you, and if he thinks you have been so near the place and haven't been to see him, I'm afraid he'll be hurt."

Frank looked undecided a moment, and I glanced at him anxiously. Truly, I was very eager that day to secure a companion for my father.

" Father is depressed," I added. " I don't think he's quite so cheerful and hopeful as he used to be, and I am sure you would do him good."

Frank laughed. " Very well," said he, turning down the lane with me, " if your

mother is displeased, Miss Margaret, let it
be on your head."

" Oh, I'm not afraid of mother," I said,
although in truth I was very much afraid of
her. "She will be pleased enough if you
cheer up father. And if you tell him some
good news of his plan about the poor little
children, you will cheer him up."

" He mustn't set his heart too much upon
that just at present," said Frank, in a cool,
business-like kind of way. " There's a deal
of hard, patient work to be done at that
before it'll take any shape, you know."

" Yes, I understand," said I ; " but who
is going to do the work ? "

He looked a bit put out for the moment,
but he said cheerily—" Ah, that's just it.
We must find the proper man—the man for
the place. Then it'll go like a house on fire."
And then he turned and fixed his brown eyes
on me, as was his wont, and said, " But how
is it that this bailiff hasn't roused your father's
heart in his own work more, and made him
forget these outside schemes ? "

I flushed with anger. I thought the remark unjustifiable.

" I hear he's a clever fellow," continued the Captain. " That's it, I suppose. He prefers to go his own gait. Although they tell me "—he said this as if he were paying me a compliment—" they tell me *you* can twist him round your little finger."

" Who are they?" cried I, my lip trembling. " They had best mind their own business."

He laughed gaily. " The same as ever, I see," he said. " But you might well be proud of such a feat. He struck me as a tough customer the only time I saw him."

I set my lips tight together and refused to answer another word ; but when we had left the pines and turned out of the lane into the road, I was sorry for him, and forgave him—for, glancing at him, I saw that his cheek was quite pale.

" I'm dreadfully afraid of your parents," laughed he. " Your mother won't deign to shake hands with me, and your father will be hurt because I haven't brought a train of little London waifs at my heels."

Of course it was neither the prospect of mother's cold welcome, nor the thought of father's disappointment at the stagnation of

the scheme, which had really made his cheek
white. I understood things better than that.
It was that he was going to see Joyce, whom
he had not seen for three months. I was
sorry for the poor fellow, in spite of his
having offended me.

On the top of my original plan, which had
only been to get him to the Grange, another
took sudden shape. It was a Thursday—
dairy morning. But as we had come down
the street, I had seen mother's tall back beside the counter of the village-grocer's shop,
and I determined to risk Deborah's presence,
and to bring Frank straight in through the
back-door to the milk-pans and Joyce's face.

Luck favoured me. Deborah had gone
outside to rinse some vessel not quite to her
mind, and Joyce stood alone with a fresh
pink frock and a fresh fair face against the
white tiles, kneading the butter with sleeves
upturned. I left Frank there, and ran on to
Deborah, who showed signs of returning.

" Whatever does that dandified young beau
want round about again?" said she. "I thought
he had taken those handsome calves of his
to London to make love to the ladies."

I must mention that Frank always wore a knickerbocker suit down at Marshlands,— a costume less in vogue ten years ago than it is now, and an affectation which found no favour in Deborah's sight. To tell the truth, it did not please *me* that day; nothing about him quite pleased me, yet indeed I think he was the same as he had always been. But I was not going to let myself dwell upon anything that was not in the Captain's favour, and certainly I was not going to let Deborah comment upon it. After all, as I had once said to mother, he was my sister's lover, not mine; but he *was* my sister's lover, and as such I should stick up for him, through thick and thin.

"He's come to see father," said I shortly.

"That's the first time I knew that the way to your father's room was through the dairy," grinned Deborah. "But look here, Margaret,"—and here old Deb grew as solemn as a judge,—"you'd no business to bring him in there when your mother was away. You know very well you hadn't. You'll get into a scrape." How much Deb really knew about the particulars of Joyce's

engagement I have never found out, but
that she guessed what she did not know
was more than likely.

"Why not?" asked I.

"Why not? Because he's a slippery
young eel, that's why not," said Deborah.
"If Joyce cares for him, the sooner she
leaves off the better. But it's my belief
she's got more sense in her head than some
folk give her credit for."

"Of course Joyce cares for him," cried I
angrily, "and he's not slippery at all. He
can't come courting her when mother forbids
him the house. But it's very unkind of
mother, and that's why I brought him. I
don't care if I do get into a scrape for it.
You're a hard-hearted old woman to talk so.
But I suppose you've forgotten what it was
to be young—it's so long ago."

"I remember enough about it to know
how many men out of a dozen there are
that are fit to be trusted, my dear," smiled
Deborah grimly. "And my old ears haven't
grown so queer yet but they can tell a jig
from a psalm tune."

"I don't think you go to church often

enough to know them apart," sneered I ; for
Deb was not as conspicuous for piety as
Reuben, and was wont to declare that when
she listened to parson her head grew that
muddled and stagnated, she couldn't tell her
left hand from her right.

"Ah, I'm not like some folk as likes to go
and be told o' their sins," said she, alluding
as usual to the unlucky Reuben. "I know
mine well enough, and on the Sabbath I
likes to put up my legs and give my mind
to 'em in peace and quiet. But I'm not
afraid I shall hear the Old Hundredth if I
go into the dairy just now," grinned she,
catching up the milk - pail, which she had
been scrubbing viciously,—"so I'll just go
back and finish my work."

I laid my hand on her arm to detain her,
but at that moment Trayton Harrod appeared round the corner from the garden.

"Where's Reuben ?" asked he, with a
thunder-cloud upon his brow.

"That's more than I can tell you," answered
Deb shortly. "I'm not the man's keeper."

"What's the matter ?" I asked.

"Some malicious persons have been taking

the trouble to break the pipes that have just
been laid across to the new reservoir," he
answered. "They were not yet covered
in. But I'm determined to find out the
offenders."

"Well, you needn't come asking after
Reuben then," said old Deb with rough
staunchness. "The man mayn't be much
for brains, but he aint got time to plan tricks
o' that sort."

"I'm not suspecting Reuben," answered
Harrod, "but I look to Reuben to help me
to find out who's to blame."

"Well, if there's wrong been done against
master, so he will," declared Deborah again.
"Reuben's a true man to his master, say
what you may of him. You'd best not come
telling any tales of Reuben to me."

"No, no," replied Harrod hurriedly, "I
want to tell no tales of Reuben nor any one
else, but I must get to the bottom of the
matter;" and then turning to me, he added,
"I must see your father at once."

He moved across the yard to the outer
door, but midway he stopped, listening.

The voices in the dairy had attracted his

attention.   I think he was going to ask me
who was there, when suddenly Joyce came
out of the door, her cheeks red, her eyes wet
with tears.

As soon as she saw him she ran quickly
by, and round the corner of the yard to the
front of the house; but I knew by the way
that he glanced at me that he had seen
her eyes were full of tears.   He did not
speak, however, neither did he look after
her.   He first glanced across to the dairy, but
Frank Forrester did not show himself—and
he strode across to the gate of the yard and
let himself out into the road.

"I'll see your father another time," he
said to me as he went past.

I went round the corner, meaning to follow
Joyce; but remembering that Frank must be
in a very uncomfortable position, and that I
was rather bound to see him through with it,
I went back and found him bidding Deborah tell me he would come again in the
evening.

"The master'll be busy all the evening,"
she said; and her inhospitality decided me to
make a bold move.

"Father is at liberty now," I said. "Please
come this way." And he had no choice but
to follow me round to the front.

Luckily for me, father was there alone,
reading his newspaper in the few spare
minutes before dinner : neither Joyce nor
mother were visible. He welcomed Frank
even more cordially than I had hoped.

" How are you, lad ? " he cried heartily.
" Why, I didn't know you were near the
place at all. When did you come ? "

Frank sat down in his usual place, and the
two talked together just as if they had never
parted. All Frank's cautiousness, not to
say half-heartedness, about father's scheme
seemed to have evaporated, now that he
was in his presence, just as if he were
afraid or ashamed not to be as enthusiastic
as he was. As I listened to them I couldn't
believe that he had told me ten minutes before that father was "apt to be over-sanguine,"
and that he must not " set his heart too
much " upon the matter. On the contrary,
it seemed to be Frank who was sanguine,
and father who was suggesting the difficulties of working ; father, moreover, who

used almost the very phrase about its being
necessary to get the proper man to work the
details, and Frank who declared, as he had
declared before, that *he* would be the man.
How was it that, as soon as his back was
turned, the fire seemed to die out of him ?
Was he like some sort of fire-bricks that can
absorb heat, and give it out again fiercely
while the fire is around them, but that grow
dead and cold as soon as the surrounding
warmth is withdrawn ?

But it was very pleasant to see them there
talking as merrily as ever.   Merrily ?   Well,
yes, with Frank it was " merrily," but with
father I don't think it had ever been anything but earnestly, and now I fancied that
there was even a tinge of hopelessness about
him which had not been there of old.   Yet
he smiled often, and treated Frank just in
that half rough, half affectionate way that he
had always had towards him, — something
protecting, something humorous,—almost as
though he traced in him a streak of weakness, but could not help being fascinated by
the bright kindliness, the sympathetic desire
to please in spite of himself.

Perhaps it was so with all of us,—with all
of us, excepting mother. She had never felt
the fascination, she had always seen straight
through the mirror. And as she had always
been inexorable, so she was inexorable that
day.

Father, in his eagerness about the interest
that he had at heart, had forgotten all about
Joyce, all about the reason why Frank
Forrester should not be at the Grange.
But I had not forgotten it; I knew mother
would not have forgotten it, and I stood—
with a trembling heart—listening for her step
upon the stairs within.

She came at last, and one glance at her
face told me that Frank's presence was no
surprise to her; that she knew of it, and
knew of it from Joyce. Her lips were
pressed together half nervously, her blue
eyes were smaller than usual; and she
rustled her dress as she walked, which somehow always seemed to me a sure sign of dis-
pleasure in her. She did not hold out her
hand-to him, although he advanced with every
show of cordiality to greet her as usual.

"Oh, Mrs Maliphant, you are angry with

me for coming here," cried he, in a half
humorous, half appealing voice, that he was
wont to use when he wanted to conciliate.
"You're quite right. What can I say for
myself?"

He did not say that I had persuaded him.
I liked him for that, but I said it for him.

"*I* brought Captain Forrester here, mother,"
said I in my boldest manner, trying neither
to blush nor to let my voice quaver. "I
knew father would want to see him, and he
is only in Marshlands for one day."

"Captain Forrester is always welcome in
my house," said father, and his voice did
shake a little, but whether from annoyance
or distress it was not possible to tell. But
mother said nothing. She kept her hands
folded in front of her. It was Joyce who
spoke — Joyce who had followed mother
down the stairs and out into the porch.

"Father, I have been telling mother," said
she, coming very close to him, "that I knew
nothing of Captain Forrester's coming here
to-day. I did not wish to see him."

She kept her head bent as she said the
words, but she said them quite firmly, al-

though in a low voice.   Certainly Joyce, for
a gentle and diffident girl, had a wonderful
trick of courage at times.   I admired her for
it, although to - night she angered me : she
might have allowed her love to shine forth a
little—for her lover's sake if not for her own.

"All right, my girl," answered father, without looking at her.   "I understand."

And then he turned again to Frank.
"You'll stay and have a bit of dinner with
us?" he said.

I was grateful to him for saying it, for
things were altogether rather uncomfortable.
The honest frankness of our family is a
characteristic of which I am proud, but it
certainly has its uncomfortable side.   Fortunately Captain Forrester's pleasant and easy
manners were second nature, and cost him no
trouble.   They came to the aid of us all that
day.

"Oh, Mrs Maliphant does not echo that
kind invitation of yours," said he.   "I know
I have deserved her wrath.   A bargain is a
bargain."   He put out his hand again.   "But
she will shake hands with me before I go?"
he added.

Who could have resisted him? Mother put out her hand.

"You're welcome to our board, Captain, if you will stay," said she.

"Thank you, that is kind of you," answered he, with real feeling in his voice. " I mustn't stay, I am due elsewhere, but I appreciate your asking me none the less."

He turned to me and shook hands with me warmly. Then he stopped in front of Joyce.

She did not lift her eyes; she put her hand silently into his outstretched palm, without, so far as I could see, the slightest tremor. He pressed the soft long fingers in his for a moment, and then he turned away without speaking.

Father and he went along the passage together, talking — and it was father who showed him out of the front door.

I was sorry that I had persuaded him to come to the Grange. Harrod had seen Joyce in tears, and would wonder what was the cause; and was it worth while to have gone through the very uncomfortable scene which had just taken

place for anything that had been gained ?
It was Joyce's own fault, but it showed
me how idle it was to hope to move her
in any line of conduct which she had laid
out for herself.

CHAPTER XXVIII.

THE next morning I was still more sorry
that I had brought Frank to the Grange.

Mother very rightly upbraided me for it,
and in a way that showed me that she was
more than ever determined that Joyce should
not marry Captain Forrester if she could
help it. She said that Joyce was beginning
to forget this dandy love-affair, and that it
was all the more annoying of me to have
gone putting my finger in the pie and stirring up old memories. I declared that Joyce
was not forgetting Frank at all, and told
mother I wondered at her for thinking a
daughter of hers could be so fickle, and for
supposing that her manner meant anything
but the determination to keep to the unfair
promise that had been extracted from her.

Ah, dear me, if I could have believed in

that other string that mother had to her bow
for Joyce! But although the Squire came to
the Grange just as often as ever, I could not
deceive myself into thinking his coming or
going made any difference to my sister, whatever might be his feelings towards her. If
Joyce had not encouraged her lover, as I
thought she ought to have done, that was
not the reason. I told myself that the reason
was in the different way in which we looked
at such matters, but I was sorry I had
brought Frank to the Grange.

With my arrogance of youth, I might have
got over mother's scolding if I could have
persuaded myself that I had done any good,
but I could not but think that I seemed to
have done nothing but harm. Joyce was
almost distant to me in a way that had never
happened before in our lives; and when I
tried to upbraid her for her coldness, she
choked me off in a quiet fashion that there
was no withstanding and left me alone, sore
and silent and angry. Oh, and there was a
worse result of that unlucky visit than all
this, although I would not even tell my own
heart of it.

Joyce, as I have said, was moody and silent all the next day. To be sure the weather had turned from that glorious heat to a dull-grey showery fit that was most depressing to everybody. It had most reason to be depressing to Trayton Harrod, who had his eye on the crops even more anxiously than father had himself. The rain had not as yet been heavy or continuous enough to do more than refresh the parched earth, but a little more might make a serious difference to the wheat and the hops, of which the one harvest was not yet all garnered, the second nearly ready for picking.

This and the annoyance about the broken water-pipes—in which matter he had failed to discover the offenders—was quite enough, of course, to account for the cloud upon the bailiff's brow as I came across him that evening on the ridge of the downs by the new reservoir. I ought to have remembered this; I ought to have soothed the trouble ; I should have done so a fortnight ago. But I was ruffled, unreasonable, unjust.

" Well, have you discovered anything more about that ridiculous affair?" I asked, nipping

off the twig of a bush in the hedge pettishly
as I spoke.

"What affair?" asked he, although I knew
that he knew perfectly well what I meant.

"Well, about those water-pipes that you
fancy the men have stamped upon to spite
you," laughed I ill-naturedly.

He pressed his lips together. "I think I
guess pretty well who was at the bottom of
it," he said. "But the work is finished now
and in working order, so I shall say no more
about it."

I knew very well that, if he could have
been certain of his facts, he would have said
a great deal more about it, and in my unreasonable ill-temper I wanted to make him
feel this.

"Guessing isn't enough," I replied. "But
if you could be sure, it would be far better to
let the man know that you have discovered
him. You'll never get anything out of these
Sussex people by knuckling under to them."

I was sorry for the words as soon as I had
said them, for it was an insulting speech to a
man in his position, but I wouldn't show any
humility.

"Thank you," he answered coldly. "I must do the best I can, of course, in managing the Sussex people. But, anyhow, it is *I* who have to do it."

I would not see the just reproof. "Well, if any one is to blame in this it isn't poor old Reuben," I declared stoutly; "he's obstinate, but he isn't mean. It *might* be Jack Barnstaple. I don't say it is, but it *might* be. It isn't Reuben."

"I am quite of your opinion," answered he. "But, as you say, guessing is of no avail, so we had best let the matter drop."

He turned to go one way and I the other. But just as we were parting, Reuben appeared upon the crest of the hill with Luck at his heels. They were inseparable companions. Luck was the one sign of his former calling that still clung to poor old Reuben. But he was very old—older than his master; both had done good work in their day, but both were nearly past work now.

"That dog will have to be shot soon," said Trayton Harrod, looking at the way the poor beast dragged itself along, stiff with rheuma-

tism, which the damp weather had brought
out.   " I told Reuben so the other day."

"Shot!" cried I, with angry eyes. " No
one shall shoot that dog while I have a word
to say in the matter."

And I ran across to where Luck was coming to meet me, his tail wagging with pleasure.

" Poor old Luck! poor old fellow!" I
murmured, stooping to caress him. " They
want to shoot you, do they? But I won't
allow it."

" Shoot him!" growled Reuben, looking
round to the bailiff, who had followed me.
" Shoot my dog!"

" He's not *your* dog, Reuben," I said.
" He's father's, although you have had him
for your own so long.   And father will have
a voice in the matter before he's shot. Don't
be afraid.   He shan't be shot. We can
nurse him when he needs nursing, and he
shall die peaceably like a human being. He
deserves as much any day, I'm sure. He has
worked as well."

Taff was my special dog, and it was true
that Luck had always, as it were, belonged
to Reuben; but now that I fancied him in

danger, all my latent love of the weak and injured rose up strong within me, and I fought for the post of Luck's champion. Perhaps my mood of unreasonable temper had just a little to do with it too.

"You are mistaken," said Trayton coldly. "The poor beast is ill and weary. It would be a far greater kindness to shoot him."

" Well, he *shan't* be shot, then, so there's an end," cried I testily, rising to my feet and looking Harrod in the face.

"Oh, very good ; of course it's not my business," said he.

He turned away up the slope. But the spirit of annoyance was in Reuben as it was in me that day.

" I came to have a bit of a look at the 'op fields, master," said he. " The sky don't look just as we might choose, do it ? "

"This rain is not enough to hurt," growled Harrod, without looking round.

"No, no; we might put up with this so long as it don't go on," agreed Reuben. slowly. "We want a bit of rain after all that dry weather. You didn't get your water - pipes laid on in time for the dry

weather—did you, Master Harrod? begging
your pardon," asked the old man slily.

"No; some mischievous persons took a
childish delight in putting them out of order,"
said the bailiff, turning round sharply. " But
I have my eye on them."

" They're dreadful brittle things, them china
things for such work," said Reuben in a slow,
sleepy voice. " I doubt you'll never get the
water to go just as you fancy. They do say
there's another broke down by Widow
Dawes'," he added with a grin.

Harrod turned round with a muttered im-
precation.

" But there, I'm thinking you won't want
no water round about for some while to
come, mister. The Lord 'll do it for ye."

" I tell you the weather hasn't broken up,
man. This rain is nothing," growled Harrod
again, striding up the bank as he spoke.

" Right, right," agreed Reuben, nodding
his head. " We must trust the Lord, we
must. Though, for my part, I'd sooner trust
Him with anything rather than a few gardens
of 'ops." Reuben sighed as he looked out
across the valley that was so rich now with

the tall and graceful growths. "They're a
fine sight now," said he, "but the Lord can
lay 'em low." And with that comforting
reflection he turned his back on me, and
went down the path.

Luckily for Reuben, I had not leisure just
then to think of him or his words ; my thoughts
were elsewhere. Trayton Harrod had reached
the top of the slope. He was nearly out of
ear-shot. I watched his figure grow longer
and longer upon the softening sky that was
slowly clearing with the coming twilight.

How could I bear to let him go from me
like that ? Was it for this that we had
had those good times together—those happy,
happy hours, that lived in my memory like
stars upon a bright sky ? Was it for nothing
that he had held my hands in his and tuned
his voice to gentleness in speaking to me ?
Was it for nothing that my heart beat wild
and hot, so full of longing, so full of devotion ? Oh, and yet it was I who had made
this foolish quarrel. How could I have allowed my unreasonable temper to get the
better of me like that ? It was my fault,
all my fault ! What devil had taken pos-

session of me to fill my heart with wicked and unjust fancies, to embitter all that was but a little while ago so sweet?

My heart was heavy, the tears came into my eyes. If he loved me he would forgive me, I said to myself, and I forgot all of what I had been wont to consider proper pride, and ran after him.

"Mr Harrod," I called. He turned at once and waited for me. "You're going to London one of these days, aren't you?" I said breathlessly, for I had run up the bank.

"One day before the hop-picking begins," he said hurriedly, impatient to get on; "but not before the harvest is all in."

He turned, walking on, and I walked by his side.

"Well, when you go, I want you to do something for me," I said. "I want you to buy some books for me."

"Buy some books!" ejaculated he. "What books?"

"I don't know," I answered. "I have saved some money, and I want to buy some books with it. But I don't know what books. I thought you would advise me."

He laughed. "I don't think I'm at all the proper person to advise you what books to buy. I'm not much of a reader myself. I've got my father's books, and have had some pleasant hours with them too, but I don't know if they're the best kind of books for a young woman to read. No, I'm not the proper person to advise you, I'm sure. You'd better ask the Squire."

"The Squire!" cried I, vexed. "And pray, why should I ask the Squire?"

"Well, he's an older friend of yours than I am, and far better suited to advise you," answered Harrod. "And he would do anything for you, I'm sure."

Was it possible that Harrod might be under a delusion? Somehow it gave me pleasure to think that it might be possible.

"The Squire is no friend of mine," said I. I was ashamed of the words before they were spoken, they were so untrue; but I spoke them under the smart of the moment.

"How can you say such a thing!" said Harrod sternly.

"I don't mean to say that he wouldn't do anything for any of us," I murmured,

ashamed.   " I only meant · to say that
he would be more likely to do it — for
Joyce."

I felt his eyes turn upon me, and I raised
mine to his face.   It was quiet, all trace of
the temper that had been there five minutes
ago had vanished, but his eyes, those steely-
grey eyes, looked me through.   But it was
only for a moment.   Then the shade upon
his brow melted away, and the hard lines of
his mouth broke into that parting of the
lips which was scarcely a smile, yet lit his
whole face as with a strong, sharp ray of
light.

There never was a face that changed as
his face changed ; not with many and vary-
ing expressions as with some folk,—for his
was a character reserved almost to isolation,
and if he felt many things he told but few of
them, either tacitly or in words,—but with a
slow melting, from something that was almost
akin to cruelty into something that was very
much akin to good, honest tenderness.   It
was as the breaking of sunlight across some
rugged rock where the shadow has hidden
every possible pathway : when the sunlight

came, one could see that there was a way to ascend. Judging with the dispassionateness of distance, I think that Harrod feared any such thing as feeling. Life was a straight-forward and not necessarily pleasant road, which must be travelled doggedly, without pausing by the way, without stopping to think if there were any means by which it might be made more agreeable : life was all work for Trayton Harrod.

And as a natural consequence, if he had any feelings he instinctively avoided dwell-ing on the fact; therefore he mistrusted any expression of them in others. He was cruel, but if he was cruel to others he was also cruel to himself.

That evening, however, the sunshine broke out across the rock. It melted the last morsel of pride in me. He turned away his eyes again without a word, after that long, half-amused, half reproachful, and wholly kind look. It puzzled me a little, and yet it gave me courage.

" I think I'm in a very bad temper to-day," said I, with a little awkward laugh. " I think I was very rude to you just now."

"Rude!" echoed he, turning to me quickly.
"Why, when were you rude?"

"Just now, about the hops and everything."

He laughed aloud, quite merrily. "Good
gracious! surely we are good friends enough
to stand a sharp word or two," cried he.

I was silent. Harrod walked very fast,
and talking was difficult. When he reached
the top of the hill he held out his hand and
said, in a cheerful matter-of-fact voice, "Good
night; I must be getting along to Widow
Dawes' as fast as I can."

I stood watching him as he ran down the
slope. At any other time I should have been
just as much excited as he was about the
breakage of the pipes, but that night there
was a dull emptiness about things for which
I had no reason.

The west was still clouded, and in the plains
the struggling rays of the sinking sun made
golden spray of the mists that the rain had
left. But to the eastward the sky was clear
of showers.

The mill was quite still, its warning arms
were silent; it stood white upon the flaxen

slope where the short grass was burnt to chaff by the rare summer heat,—white and huge against the twilight blue. Behind it—slowly, slowly out of the blue sea—rose the golden August moon.

I turned my back to the clouds and faced the golden moon.

END OF THE SECOND VOLUME

PRINTED BY WILLIAM BLACKWOOD AND SONS.